The Matchmaker

The Matchmaker

A Farce in Four Acts

Thornton Wilder

HARPER PERENNIAL

NEW YORK • LONDON • TORONTO • SYDNEY • NEW DELHI • AUCKLAND

FIRST HARPER PERENNIAL EDITION PUBLISHED 2017.

Library of Congress Cataloging-in-Publication Data has been applied for.

ISBN 978-0-06-269349-5 (pbk.)

17 18 19 20 21   LSC   10 9 8 7 6 5 4 3 2 1

Contents

Contents

Introduction

—∽—

Thornton Wilder's *The Matchmaker* is that rarest of birds: a virtually perfect stage comedy. Indeed, along with Hecht and MacArthur's *The Front Page* and Kaufman and Hart's *You Can't Take It With You*, it is one of the three or four greatest American comedies of the twentieth century.

Successfully creating timeless comedy for the stage is an art of enormous rarity. Shakespeare and Shaw managed it over ten times each. After that, the roll call includes Farquhar, Goldsmith, Sheridan, O'Keeffe, A. W. Pinero, Wilde, and Coward. And among that number we can count Wilder's *The Matchmaker*.

The play started life with a different title, *The Merchant of Yonkers*, and when it opened on Broadway in 1938, directed by the famous Max Reinhardt, it failed with the critics and closed quickly. Then, sixteen years later, something remarkable happened: the play reopened in a slightly altered version with a new director and cast, and it was a triumph, traveling from the Edinburgh Festival to London, then back to New York in a resurrection of a scope heretofore known only to the Christian religion, and certainly unprecedented in the history of Broadway. It is a testament not only to Wilder's faith in the play but also to the quality of the play itself.

So how did Wilder do it? How did he write this mini miracle of construction, high spirits, and emotional wallop?

I've spent a great deal of my writing life thinking about the structure and content of stage comedy in the English language, from *Twelfth Night* to *One Man, Two Guvnors*, and I've concluded that in order to write a good one, you need four ingredients: a strong premise, a solid structure, wit, and resonance. *The Matchmaker* has all of these in abundance.

As for premise, *The Matchmaker* has not one but two strong story lines. The first is about two country mice who escape to the big city for a day of adventure. The mice in question, Cornelius Hackl and Barnaby Tucker, are clerks in a dry goods store in the small town of Yonkers, New York, in the early 1880s. When their employer, Horace Vandergelder, tells them he'll be away for the day, they resolve to spend that day living large in New York City so that they'll have a past to remember in the years ahead. In the end, the day of adventure changes their lives forever.

The second story concerns a middle-aged heroine named Dolly Levi who yearns for a second chance at life. She gets it by coming to terms with the memory of her late husband, then marrying a lovable curmudgeon, Horace Vandergelder, who can give her something to look forward to.

Wilder based the first of these plots on a comedy titled *Einen Jux will er sich machen*, written in 1842 by the popular Viennese playwright Johann Nestroy. Comedy, even more than tragedy and melodrama, seems to require a strong premise, and the greatest playwrights have often looked backwards, seeking plots in the works of their literary forebears. Shakespeare was the master of borrowed plots, and Wilder did it several times in his career.

In 1932, Wilder adapted a German translation of the successful, contemporary Hungarian comedy *The Bride of Torozko* by Ottó Indig. The lively story is set in a small village in Eastern Europe and concerns a spunky young woman who discovers, just before she's about to be married, that she's Jewish—and during the course of the play she falls *in* love with her Jewish roots and *out* of love with her anti-Semitic fiancé. (Wilder, of mostly Protestant stock, liked to remind people that one of his ancestors was Jewish.)

Sometime before 1939, Wilder was asked by two notable Broadway producers to do an adaptation of a play with another strong storyline, *The Beaux' Stratagem*, a late Restoration comedy by George Farquhar. It concerns two down-on-their-luck city bucks who travel to the countryside to find rich wives; and as they travel from town to town, they switch identities as servant and master. Wilder abandoned the adaptation halfway through. Lucky me, a few years ago I was asked by the Wilder estate to finish it, and it has been playing in theaters around the country ever since. Knowing the original Farquhar play and Wilder adaptation as well as I do, I can see with absolute clarity why Wilder agreed to refashion the original play: because the backbone of the story is as strong as an oak. It has just the kind of sturdy, specific plot that a classic comedy needs.

As for the Dolly Levi portion of the plot, it was invented by Wilder from whole cloth. That said, it has strong roots in two traditions of comic drama that Wilder knew well. First, it tips its hat to Molière, particularly in Act One where Dolly tempts Vandergelder with the domestic delights of Ernestina Simple, using dialogue from Molière's *L'Avare*. Second, Dolly herself is in the great tradition of comic servants and factotums who save the day, her most obvious forebear being Figaro in *The Barber of Seville*. Like Figaro, Dolly has a number of skills that she markets with glee (she sells hosiery, gives guitar lessons, reduces varicose veins), and, like Figaro, she arranges marriages. In these homages to Molière and Beaumarchais (and thereby to Plautus and Shakespeare), Wilder acknowledges the debt he owes to the comic tradition that has come before him. As Wilder himself once said: "Literature has always more resembled a torch race than a furious dispute among heirs."

In one of his typical moments of modesty, Wilder put it this way: "I am not an innovator, but a rediscoverer of forgotten goods." Well, yes and no. Yes, *The Matchmaker* is a tip of the hat to the Ye Liberty Playhouse plays of Wilder's youth; yes, the one-act plays and *Our Town* owe a debt to Shakespeare, as well as, to a lesser extent, Japanese Noh drama; and yes, as A. R. Gurney has observed, Wilder shared a belief with Sophocles, Shakespeare, and George Bernard Shaw in the ability of the human struggle to circumvent the Olympic order of things. But despite his own statements to the contrary, Wilder wasn't merely a rediscoverer, he was one of the greatest innovators in the history of American drama.

Turning to structure, Wilder had a lot to draw on. He was an intellectual at heart who knew the history of drama as well as anyone of his generation. He started early, hiding in the back rows of local theaters, and one of his hobbies in later life was dating the hundreds of plays of Lope de Vega. As he said once in an interview:

> I would always advise any young writer for the theater to do everything—to adapt plays, to translate plays, to hang around theaters, to paint scenery, to become an actor. . . . There's a bottomless pit in the acquisition of how to tell an imagined story to listeners and viewers.

The Matchmaker is a masterpiece of plotting. A play needs an overall arc of action—at least the kind of play that Wilder loved—and each *act* of a comedy needs the same sort of arc. Just look at how Wilder handles this in *The Matchmaker*. Act One opens with Vandergelder juggling the demands of family and business, and it ends with an explosion of canned goods as his employees declare their day of freedom. Act Two opens with a sensible woman vowing to marry a man she doesn't love and ends with a song by the man she's beginning to love as they stand on the brink of the biggest night of their lives. Act Three opens quietly as Vandergelder instructs a waiter on how to serve him a sensible dinner and ends in comic chaos that is full of discoveries.

MRS. LEVI:

Well, there's your life, Mr. Vandergelder! Without niece—without clerks—without bride—and without your purse. *Will you marry me now?*

VANDERGELDER:

No!

MRS. LEVI:

Damn!!

THE CURTAIN FALLS

Wilder was a "playwright" in the true sense of the word. He was a *wright*, a craftsman, a writer who feels a kinship to the shipwright and the wheelwright and all the other *wrights* whose livelihoods depend on training and technique.

Wilder was also a master of a second kind of comic structure: he built his play on certain traditional comic motifs, some of which were established by Plautus, others of which were invented by Shakespeare. By my count, there are about twelve basic motifs, or themes, that recur again and again in comedies down through the ages, and *The Matchmaker* contains quite a handful of them.

One of the foremost of these is when the older generation tries to stand in the way of the sexual urges of the younger generation, and Wilder pounces on it in the very first line of the play. The lights come up and Vandergelder, who is getting a shave, declares to a young man standing nearby:

VANDERGELDER:
Loudly.

I tell you for the hundredth time, you will never marry my niece.

Did Wilder know *A Midsummer Night's Dream*, *She Stoops to Conquer*, and *The Rivals* like the back of his hand? You bet he did. This is no coincidence.

Other time-honored comic motifs that Wilder drew upon include that of the country mice going to the big city (compare *The Taming of the Shrew*, *Pots of Money*), the bickering couple who end up together (*Much Ado About Nothing*, *Private Lives*), the older man who desires a young wife (*The School for Scandal*, *London Assurance*), the wily servant who saves the day (*A Servant of Two Masters*, *One Man, Two Guvnors*), and on it goes with at least three or four more motifs clearly in evidence. Wilder turned *The Matchmaker* into a master class of comic themes.

As for the element of wit, *The Matchmaker* abounds in verbal virtuosity on every page. Five lines after Vandergelder's opening gambit, Joe the barber says, "Mr. Vandergelder, will you please sit still one minute? If I cut your throat it'll be practically unintentional." Four pages later, Wilder layers two great lines on top of each other:

VANDERGELDER:

A man's not worth a cent until he's forty. We just pay 'em wages to make mistakes—don't we, Joe?

JOE:

You almost lost an ear on it, Mr. Vandergelder.

In his first soliloquy, Vandergelder opines: "Marriage is a bribe to make a housekeeper think she's a householder." And my favorite of all is in Act Three when an apoplectic Vandergelder hires the Cabman to try to stop his niece Ermengarde from eloping with her boyfriend. The Cabman responds calmly: "Oh I know them, sir. They'll win in the end. Rivers don't run uphill."

Here, in just four words, Wilder tells us all we need to know about the unstoppable determination of love and youth. *"Rivers don't run uphill."* It reminds me of the beauty of Puck's lines in *A Midsummer Night's Dream* when the lovers finally, inevitably, come together: *"Jack shall have Jill, / Naught shall go ill, / The man shall have his mare again and all shall be well."*

As for the resonance of the play, it has the ping of a Stradivarius in the way all great plays do, by a sort of alchemy made up of all the right elements. It's concise, it's specific, it's universal, it's observant, it's entertaining, it's sparkling, it's challenging, and it's reassuring, all at once. It is set in a time and place where we'd all like to live, and the very names of the characters evoke the spirit of the play: Cornelius Hackl, Barnaby Tucker, Ermengarde, Ernestina Simple, Minnie Fay. These are fairytale names with a knowing smile.

Wilder has a lot to say in *The Matchmaker* and his serious themes are woven seamlessly into the farcical horseplay. The value of money to cure social ills is a theme that Dolly herself expands on several times in the play. Another theme, as

Wilder describes it, is "the aspiration of human beings" for a "fuller, freer participation in life." Young Barnaby sums up this key theme at the end of the play with disarming simplicity when he addresses the audience directly and says: "We all hope that in your lives you have just the right amount of sitting quietly at home, and just the right amount of . . . adventure. Goodnight!"

Wilder was wary of imposing themes too explicitly in his plays and he admired Shakespeare above all other playwrights for being profound without grinding axes. In an interview with *The Paris Review*, he said:

> [A]ll the great dramatists, except the very great-est one, have precisely employed the stage to con-vey a moral or religious point of view concerning the action. The theater is supremely fitted to say: "Behold! These things are." Yet most dramatists employ it to say: "This moral truth can be learned from beholding this action.". . . Only in Shakespeare are we free of hearing axes grind.

In the end—and this may explain why I love it so much— *The Matchmaker* is a genuine, good-hearted, good-natured *comedy* and there simply aren't enough of them in the world's repertoire. As a species, we have a tendency to wallow in our tragedies, often at the expense of those kinder spirits that put us back on our feet when we need a helping hand. Yes, all those thunderous theatrical ordeals are heart-stopping, yes, they're cathartic, yes, they make us suffer, and sometimes we're the better for it. But my loyalty is to those works of art that make my heart take wing. Jane Austen puts it this way at the end of *Mansfield Park*:

Let other pens dwell on guilt and misery. I quit such odious subjects as soon as I can, impatient to restore everybody, not greatly in fault themselves, to tolerable comfort, and to have done with all the rest.

Wilder himself puts it best of all:

Anybody can make a comedy which is cruel. It is very hard to make a comedy which is kind. To give a fellow feeling between the young and old, that is art.

And that is *The Matchmaker*.

KEN LUDWIG
Wesley Heights, Washington, D.C.

Ken Ludwig is a two-time Olivier Award–winning playwright whose work has been performed in more than thirty countries in over twenty languages. He has written twenty-four plays and musicals, among them *Lend Me A Tenor*, which won two Tony Awards, *Crazy For You*, which won the Tony Award for Best Musical, *Moon Over Buffalo*, and *Baskerville*. His shows have had six productions on Broadway and seven in London's West End. His book *How To Teach Your Children Shakespeare* is published by Random House.

The Merchant of Yonkers was produced by Herman Shumlin and directed by Max Reinhardt. The production was designed by Boris Aronson. The cast included Jane Cowl, June Walker, Nydia Westman, Minna Phillips, Percy Waram, Tom Ewell, John Call, Joseph Sweeney, Philip Coolidge, and Edward Nannery. It was first performed on December 12, 1938, at the Colonial Theatre, Boston. The New York engagement opened at the Guild Theatre on December 28, 1938.

The Matchmaker was produced for the Edinburgh Festival by Tennent Productions. It was directed by Dr. Tyrone Guthrie, and the production was designed by Tanya Moiseiwitsch. The first performance was at the Royal Lyceum Theatre, Edinburgh, on August 23, 1954.

The same production opened at the Theatre Royal, Haymarket, London, on November 4, 1954. Without changes in the principal roles—with the exception of that of Mr. Vandergelder, which was played successively by Sam Levene, Eddie Mayehoff, and Loring Smith—the play was performed at the Locust Street Theatre, Philadelphia, on October 27, 1955.

The cast of the play from Edinburgh to New York, with the exceptions noted, included:

HORACE VANDERGELDER	Loring Smith
CORNELIUS HACKL	Arthur Hill
BARNABY TUCKER	Robert Morse
	(following Alec McCowen)
MALACHI STACK	Patrick McAlinney
AMBROSE KEMPER	Alexander Davion
	(following Lee Montague)
WAITERS	William Lanteau
	(following and followed
	by Timothy Findley)
	and John Milligan
CABMAN	Peter Bayliss
DOLLY LEVI	Ruth Gordon
IRENE MOLLOY	Eileen Herlie
MINNIE FAY	Rosamund Greenwood
ERMENGARDE	Prunella Scales
GERTRUDE	Charity Grace
	(following Henzie Raeburn)
FLORA VAN HUYSEN	Esme Church
COOK	Christine Thomas
	(following Daphne Newton)

This play is a rewritten version of *The Merchant of Yonkers*, which was directed in 1938 by Max Reinhardt and is again dedicated to Max Reinhardt with deep admiration and indebtedness.

CHARACTERS

HORACE VANDERGELDER	*A merchant of Yonkers, New York*
CORNELIUS HACKL BARNABY TUCKER MALACHI STACK	*Clerks in his store*
AMBROSE KEMPER	*An artist*
JOE SCANLON	*A barber*
RUDOLPH AUGUST	*Waiters*
A CABMAN	
MRS. DOLLY LEVI MISS FLORA VAN HUYSEN	*Friends of Vandergelder's late wife*
MRS. IRENE MOLLOY	*A milliner*
MINNIE FAY	*Her assistant*
ERMENGARD	*Vandergelder's niece*
GERTRUDE	*Vandergelder's housekeeper*
MISS VAN HUYSEN'S COOK	

TIME: 1880s.
Act I. Vandergelder's house in Yonkers, New York.
Act II. Mrs. Molloy's hat shop, New York.
Act III. The Harmonia Gardens Restaurant
on the Battery, New York.
Act IV. Miss Van Huysen's house, New York.

This play is based upon a comedy by Johann Nestroy, *Einen Jux will er sich machen* (Vienna, 1842), which was in turn based upon an English original, *A Day Well Spent* (London, 1835) by John Oxenford.

Act I

Living room of Mr. Vandergelder's house, over his hay, feed and provision store in Yonkers, fifteen miles north of New York City. Articles from the store have overflowed into this room; it has not been cleaned for a long time and is in some disorder, but it is not sordid or gloomy.

There are three entrances. One at the center back leads into the principal rooms of the house. One on the back right (all the directions are from the point of view of the actors) opens on steps which descend to the street door. One on the left leads to Ermengarde's room.

In the center of the room is a trap door; below it is a ladder descending to the store below.

Behind the trap door and to the left of it is a tall accountant's desk; to the left of it is an old-fashioned stove with a stovepipe going up into the ceiling. Before the desk is a tall stool. On the right of the stage is a table with some chairs about it.

Mr. Vandergelder's Gladstone bag, packed for a journey, is beside the desk.

It is early morning.

VANDERGELDER, sixty, choleric, vain and sly, wears a soiled dressing gown. He is seated with a towel about his neck, in a chair beside the desk, being shaved by JOE SCANLON.

VANDERGELDER is smoking a cigar and holding a hand mirror. AMBROSE KEMPER is angrily striding about the room.

VANDERGELDER:

Loudly.

I tell you for the hundredth time you will never marry my niece.

AMBROSE:

Thirty; dressed as an "artist."

And I tell you for the thousandth time that I will marry your niece; and right soon, too.

VANDERGELDER:

Never!

AMBROSE:

Your niece is of age, Mr. Vandergelder. Your niece has consented to marry me. This is a free country, Mr. Vandergelder—not a private kingdom of your own.

VANDERGELDER:

There are no free countries for fools, Mr. Kemper. Thank you for the honor of your visit—good morning.

JOE:

Fifty; lanky, mass of gray hair falling into his eyes.

Mr. Vandergelder, will you please sit still one minute? If I cut your throat it'll be practically unintentional.

VANDERGELDER:

Ermengarde is not for you, nor for anybody else who can't support her.

AMBROSE:

I tell you I can support her. I make a very good living.

VANDERGELDER:

No, sir! A living is made, Mr. Kemper, by selling something that everybody needs at least once a year. Yes, sir! And a million is made by producing something that everybody needs every day. You artists produce something that nobody needs at any time. You may sell a picture once in a while, but you'll make no living. Joe, go over there and stamp three times. I want to talk to Cornelius.

JOE *crosses to trap door and stamps three times.*

AMBROSE:

Not only can I support her now, but I have considerable expectations.

VANDERGELDER:

Expectations! We merchants don't do business with them. I don't keep accounts with people who promise somehow to pay something someday, and I don't allow my niece to marry such people.

AMBROSE:

Very well, from now on you might as well know that I regard any way we can find to get married is right and fair. Ermengarde is of age, and there's no law . . .

VANDERGELDER *rises and crosses toward Ambrose.* JOE
SCANLON *follows him complainingly and tries to find a
chance to cut his hair even while he is standing.*

VANDERGELDER:

Law? Let me tell you something, Mr. Kemper: most of the people in the world are fools. The law is there to prevent crime; we men of sense are there to prevent foolishness. It's I, and not the law, that will prevent Ermengarde from marrying you, and I've taken some steps already. I've sent her away to get this nonsense out of her head.

AMBROSE:

Ermengarde's . . . not here?

VANDERGELDER:

She's gone—east, west, north, south. I thank you for the honor of your visit.

Enter GERTRUDE—*eighty; deaf; half blind; and very pleased with herself.*

GERTRUDE:

Everything's ready, Mr. Vandergelder. Ermengarde and I have just finished packing the trunk.

VANDERGELDER:

Hold your tongue!

JOE *is shaving Vandergelder's throat, so he can only wave his hands vainly.*

GERTRUDE:

Yes, Mr. Vandergelder, Ermengarde's ready to leave. Her trunk's all marked. Care Miss Van Huysen, 8 Jackson Street, New York.

VANDERGELDER:

Breaking away from Joe.

Hell and damnation! Didn't I tell you it was a secret?

AMBROSE:

Picks up hat and coat—kisses Gertrude.

Care Miss Van Huysen, 8 Jackson Street, New York. Thank you very much. Good morning, Mr. Vandergelder.

Exit AMBROSE, *to the street.*

VANDERGELDER:

It won't help you, Mr. Kemper—

To Gertrude.

Deaf! And blind! At least you can do me the favor of being dumb!

GERTRUDE:

Chk—chk! Such a temper! Lord save us!

CORNELIUS *puts his head up through the trap door. He is thirty-three; mock-deferential—he wears a green apron and is in his shirt-sleeves.*

CORNELIUS:

Yes, Mr. Vandergelder?

VANDERGELDER:

Go in and get my niece's trunk and carry it over to the station. Wait! Gertrude, has Mrs. Levi arrived yet?

CORNELIUS *comes up the trap door, steps into the room and closes the trap door behind him.*

GERTRUDE:

Don't shout. I can hear perfectly well. Everything's clearly marked.

Exit left.

VANDERGELDER:
Have the buggy brought round to the front of the store in half an hour.

CORNELIUS:
Yes, Mr. Vandergelder.

VANDERGELDER:
This morning I'm joining my lodge parade and this afternoon I'm going to New York. Before I go, I have something important to say to you and Barnaby. Good news. Fact is—I'm going to promote you. How old are you?

CORNELIUS:
Thirty-three, Mr. Vandergelder.

VANDERGELDER:
What?

CORNELIUS:
Thirty-three.

VANDERGELDER:
That all? That's a foolish age to be at. I thought you were forty.

CORNELIUS:
Thirty-three.

VANDERGELDER:
A man's not worth a cent until he's forty. We just pay 'em wages to make mistakes—don't we, Joe?

JOE:
You almost lost an ear on it, Mr. Vandergelder.

VANDERGELDER:

I was thinking of promoting you to chief clerk.

CORNELIUS:

What am I now, Mr. Vandergelder?

VANDERGELDER:

You're an impertinent fool, that's what you are. Now, if you behave yourself, I'll promote you from impertinent fool to chief clerk, with a raise in your wages. And Barnaby may be promoted from idiot apprentice to incompetent clerk.

CORNELIUS:

Thank you, Mr. Vandergelder.

VANDERGELDER:

However, I want to see you again before I go. Go in and get my niece's trunk.

CORNELIUS:

Yes, Mr. Vandergelder.

Exit CORNELIUS, *left.*

VANDERGELDER:

Joe—the world's getting crazier every minute. Like my father used to say: the horses'll be taking over the world soon.

JOE:

Presenting mirror.

I did what I could, Mr. Vandergelder, what with you flying in and out of the chair.

He wipes last of the soap from Vandergelder's face.

VANDERGELDER:

Fine, fine. Joe, you do a fine job, the same fine job you've done me for twenty years. Joe . . . I've got special reasons for looking my best today . . . isn't there something a little extry you could do, something a little special? I'll pay you right up to fifty cents—see what I mean? Do some of those things you do to the young fellas. Touch me up; smarten me up a bit.

JOE:

All I know is fifteen cents' worth, like usual, Mr. Vandergelder; and that includes everything that's decent to do to a man.

VANDERGELDER:

Now hold your horses, Joe—all I meant was . . .

JOE:

I've shaved you for twenty years and you never asked me no such question before.

VANDERGELDER:

Hold your horses, I say, Joe! I'm going to tell you a secret. But I don't want you telling it to that riffraff down to the barbershop what I'm going to tell you now. All I ask of you is a little extry because I'm thinking of getting married again; and this very afternoon I'm going to New York to call on my intended, a very refined lady.

JOE:

Your gettin' married is none of my business, Mr. Vandergelder. I done everything to you I know, and the charge is fifteen cents like it always was, and . . .

CORNELIUS *crosses, left to right, and exit, carrying a trunk on his shoulder.* ERMENGARDE *and* GERTRUDE *enter from left.*

I don't dye no hair, not even for fifty cents I don't!

VANDERGELDER:
Joe Scanlon, get out!

JOE:
And lastly, it looks to me like you're pretty rash to judge which is fools and which isn't fools, Mr. Vandergelder. People that's et onions is bad judges of who's et onions and who ain't. Good morning, ladies; good morning, Mr. Vandergelder.

Exit JOE.

VANDERGELDER:
Well, what do you want?

ERMENGARDE:
Twenty-four; pretty, sentimental.

Uncle! You said you wanted to talk to us.

VANDERGELDER:
Oh yes. Gertrude, go and get my parade regalia—the uniform for my lodge parade.

GERTRUDE:
What? Oh yes. Lord have mercy!

Exit GERTRUDE, *back center.*

VANDERGELDER:
I had a talk with that artist of yours. He's a fool.

ERMENGARDE *starts to cry.*

Weeping! Weeping! You can go down and weep for a while in New York where it won't be noticed.

He sits on desk chair, puts tie round neck and calls her over to tie it for him.

Ermengarde! I told him that when you were old enough to marry you'd marry someone who could support you. I've done you a good turn. You'll come and thank me when you're fifty.

ERMENGARDE:

But Uncle, I love him!

VANDERGELDER:

I tell you you don't.

ERMENGARDE:

But I *do!*

VANDERGELDER:

And I tell you you don't. Leave those things to me.

ERMENGARDE:

If I don't marry Ambrose I know I'll die.

VANDERGELDER:

What of?

ERMENGARDE:

A broken heart.

VANDERGELDER:

Never heard of it. Mrs. Levi is coming in a moment to take you to New York. You are going to stay two or three weeks with Miss Van Huysen, an old friend of your mother's.

GERTRUDE *re-enters with coat, sash and sword. Enter from the street, right,* MALACHI STACK.

You're not to receive any letters except from me. I'm coming to New York myself today and I'll call on you tomorrow.

To Malachi.

Who are you?

MALACHI:

Fifty. Sardonic. Apparently innocent smile; pretense of humility.

Malachi Stack, your honor. I heard you wanted an apprentice in the hay, feed, provision and hardware business.

VANDERGELDER:

An apprentice at your age?

MALACHI:

Yes, your honor; I bring a lot of experience to it.

VANDERGELDER:

Have you any letters of recommendation?

MALACHI:

Extending a sheaf of soiled papers.

Yes, indeed, your honor! First-class recommendation.

VANDERGELDER:

Ermengarde! Are you ready to start?

ERMENGARDE:

Yes.

VANDERGELDER:

Well, go and get ready some more. Ermengarde! Let me know the minute Mrs. Levi gets here.

ERMENGARDE:

Yes, Uncle Horace.

ERMENGARDE *and* GERTRUDE *exit.*

VANDERGELDER *examines the letters, putting them down one by one.*

VANDERGELDER:

I don't want an able seaman. Nor a typesetter. And I don't want a hospital cook.

MALACHI:

No, your honor, but it's all experience. Excuse me!

Selects a letter.

This one is from your former partner, Joshua Van Tuyl, in Albany.

He puts letters from table back into pocket.

VANDERGELDER:

". . . for the most part honest and reliable . . . occasionally willing and diligent." There seems to be a certain amount of hesitation about these recommendations.

MALACHI:

Businessmen aren't writers, your honor. There's only one businessman in a thousand that can write a good letter of recommendation, your honor. Mr. Van Tuyl sends his best wishes and wants to know if you can use me in the provision and hardware business.

VANDERGELDER:

Not so fast, not so fast! What's this "your honor" you use so much?

MALACHI:

Mr. Van Tuyl says you're President of the Hudson River Provision Dealers' Recreational, Musical and Burial Society.

VANDERGELDER:

I am; but there's no "your honor" that goes with it. Why did you come to Yonkers?

MALACHI:

I heard that you'd had an apprentice that was a good-for-nothing, and that you were at your wit's end for another.

VANDERGELDER:

Wit's end, wit's end! There's no dearth of good-for-nothing apprentices.

MALACHI:

That's right, Mr. Vandergelder. It's employers there's a dearth of. Seems like you hear of a new one dying every day.

VANDERGELDER:

What's that? Hold your tongue. I see you've been a barber, and a valet too. Why have you changed your place so often?

MALACHI:

Changed my place, Mr. Vandergelder? When a man's interested in experience . . .

VANDERGELDER:

Do you drink?

MALACHI:

No, thanks. I've just had breakfast.

VANDERGELDER:

I didn't ask you whether—Idiot! I asked you if you were a drunkard.

MALACHI:

No, sir! No! Why, looking at it from all sides I don't even like liquor.

VANDERGELDER:

Well, if you keep on looking at it from all sides, out you go. Remember that. Here.

Gives him remaining letters.

With all your faults, I'm going to give you a try.

MALACHI:

You'll never regret it, Mr. Vandergelder. You'll never regret it.

VANDERGELDER:

Now today I want to use you in New York. I judge you know your way around New York?

MALACHI:

Do I know New York? Mr. Vandergelder, I know every hole and corner in New York.

VANDERGELDER:

Here's a dollar. A train leaves in a minute. Take that bag to the Central Hotel on Water Street, have them save me a room. Wait for me. I'll be there about four o'clock.

MALACHI:

Yes, Mr. Vandergelder.

Picks up the bag, starts out, then comes back.

Oh, but first, I'd like to meet the other clerks I'm to work with.

VANDERGELDER:

You haven't time. Hurry now. The station's across the street.

MALACHI:

Yes, sir.

Away—then back once more.

You'll see, sir, you'll never regret it. . . .

VANDERGELDER:

I regret it already. Go on. Off with you.

Exit MALACHI, *right.*

The following speech is addressed to the audience. During it
MR. VANDERGELDER *takes off his dressing gown, puts on his*
scarlet sash, his sword and his bright-colored coat. He is
already wearing light blue trousers with a red stripe down
the sides.

VANDERGELDER:

Ninety-nine per cent of the people in the world are fools and
the rest of us are in great danger of contagion. But I wasn't
always free of foolishness as I am now. I was once young, which
was foolish; I fell in love, which was foolish; and I got married,
which was foolish; and for a while I was poor, which was more
foolish than all the other things put together. Then my wife
died, which was foolish of her; I grew older, which was sensible
of me; then I became a rich man, which is as sensible as it is rare.
Since you see I'm a man of sense, I guess you were surprised to
hear that I'm planning to get married again. Well, I've two reasons for it. In the first place, I like my house run with order,
comfort and economy. That's a woman's work; but even a
woman can't do it well if she's merely being paid for it. In order
to run a house well, a woman must have the feeling that she
owns it. Marriage is a bribe to make a housekeeper think she's

a householder. Did you ever watch an ant carry a burden twice its size? What excitement! What patience! What will! Well, that's what I think of when I see a woman running a house. What giant passions in those little bodies—what quarrels with the butcher for the best cut—what fury at discovering a moth in a cupboard! Believe me!—if women could harness their natures to something bigger than a house and a baby carriage— tck! tck!—they'd change the world. And the second reason, ladies and gentlemen? Well, I see by your faces you've guessed it already. There's nothing like mixing with women to bring out all the foolishness in a man of sense. And that's a risk I'm will- ing to take. I've just turned sixty, and I've just laid side by side the last dollar of my first half million. So if I should lose my head a little, I still have enough money to buy it back. After many years' caution and hard work, I have a right to a little risk and adventure, and I'm thinking of getting married. Yes, like all you other fools, I'm willing to risk a little security for a certain amount of adventure. Think it over.

Exit back center.

AMBROSE *enters from the street, crosses left, and whistles softly.*
ERMENGARDE *enters from left.*

ERMENGARDE:

Ambrose! If my uncle saw you!

AMBROSE:

Sh! Get your hat.

ERMENGARDE:

My hat!

AMBROSE:

Quick! Your trunk's at the station. Now quick! We're running away.

ERMENGARDE:

Running away!

AMBROSE:

Sh!

ERMENGARDE:

Where?

AMBROSE:

To New York. To get married.

ERMENGARDE:

Oh, Ambrose, I can't do that. Ambrose dear—it wouldn't be proper!

AMBROSE:

Listen. I'm taking you to my friend's house. His wife will take care of you.

ERMENGARDE:

But, Ambrose, a girl can't go on a train with a man. I can see you don't know anything about girls.

AMBROSE:

But I'm telling you we're going to get married!

ERMENGARDE:

Married! But what would *Uncle* say?

AMBROSE:

We don't care what Uncle'd say—we're eloping.

ERMENGARDE:

Ambrose Kemper! How can you use such an awful word!

AMBROSE:

Ermengarde, you have the soul of a field mouse.

ERMENGARDE:

Crying.

Ambrose, why do you say such cruel things to me?

Enter MRS. LEVI, *from the street, right. She stands listening.*

AMBROSE:

For the last time I beg you—get your hat and coat. The train leaves in a few minutes. Ermengarde, we'll get married tomorrow. . . .

ERMENGARDE:

Oh, Ambrose! I see you don't understand anything about weddings. Ambrose, don't you *respect* me?. . .

MRS. LEVI:

Uncertain age; mass of sandy hair; impoverished elegance; large, shrewd but generous nature, an assumption of worldly cynicism conceals a tireless amused enjoyment of life. She carries a handbag and a small brown paper bag.

Good morning, darling girl—how are you?

They kiss.

ERMENGARDE:

Oh, good morning, Mrs. Levi.

MRS. LEVI:

And who is this gentleman who is so devoted to you?

ERMENGARDE:

This is Mr. Kemper, Mrs. Levi. Ambrose, this is . . . . Mrs. Levi
. . . she's an old friend. . . .

MRS. LEVI:

Mrs. Levi, born Gallagher. Very happy to meet you, Mr.
Kemper.

AMBROSE:

Good morning, Mrs. Levi.

MRS. LEVI:

Mr. Kemper, *the artist!* Delighted! Mr. Kemper, may I say
something very frankly?

AMBROSE:

Yes, Mrs. Levi.

MRS. LEVI:

This thing you were planning to do is a very great mistake.

ERMENGARDE:

Oh, Mrs. Levi, please explain to Ambrose—of *course!* I want
to marry him, but to *elope!* . . . How . . .

MRS. LEVI:

Now, my dear girl, you go in and keep one eye on your uncle.
I wish to talk to Mr. Kemper for a moment. You give us a warn-
ing when you hear your Uncle Horace coming. . . .

ERMENGARDE:

Ye-es, Mrs. Levi.

Exit ERMENGARDE, *back center.*

MRS. LEVI:

Mr. Kemper, I was this dear girl's mother's oldest friend. Believe me, I am on your side. I hope you two will be married very soon, and I think I can be of real service to you. Mr. Kemper, I always go right to the point.

AMBROSE:

What is the point, Mrs. Levi?

MRS. LEVI:

Mr. Vandergelder is a very rich man, Mr. Kemper, and Ermengarde is his only relative.

AMBROSE:

But I am not interested in Mr. Vandergelder's money. I have enough to support a wife and family.

MRS. LEVI:

Enough? How much is enough when one is thinking about children and the future? The future is the most expensive luxury in the world, Mr. Kemper.

AMBROSE:

Mrs. Levi, what is the point.

MRS. LEVI:

Believe me, Mr. Vandergelder wishes to get rid of Ermengarde, and if you follow my suggestions he will even permit her to marry you. You see, Mr. Vandergelder is planning to get married himself.

AMBROSE:

What? That monster!

MRS. LEVI:

Mr. Kemper!

AMBROSE:

Married! To you, Mrs. Levi?

MRS. LEVI:

Taken aback.

Oh, no, no . . . NO! I am merely arranging it. I am helping him find a suitable bride.

AMBROSE:

For Mr. Vandergelder there are no suitable brides.

MRS. LEVI:

I think we can safely say that Mr. Vandergelder will be married to someone by the end of next week.

AMBROSE:

What are you suggesting, Mrs. Levi?

MRS. LEVI:

I am taking Ermengarde to New York on the next train. I shall not take her to Miss Van Huysen's, as is planned; I shall take her to my house. I wish you to call for her at my house at five thirty. Here is my card.

AMBROSE:

"Mrs. Dolly Gallagher Levi. Varicose veins reduced."

MRS. LEVI:

Trying to take back card.

I beg your pardon . . .

AMBROSE:

Holding card.

I beg *your* pardon. "Consultations free."

MRS. LEVI:

I meant to give you my other card. Here.

AMBROSE:

"Mrs. Dolly Gallagher Levi. Aurora Hosiery. Instruction in the guitar and mandolin." You do all these things, Mrs. Levi?

MRS. LEVI:

Two and two make four, Mr. Kemper—always did. So you will come to my house at five thirty. At about six I shall take you both with me to the Harmonia Gardens Restaurant on the Battery; Mr. Vandergelder will be there and everything will be arranged.

AMBROSE:

How?

MRS. LEVI:

Oh, I don't know. One thing will lead to another.

AMBROSE:

How do I know that I can trust you, Mrs. Levi? You could easily make our situation worse.

MRS. LEVI:

Mr. Kemper, your situation could not possibly be worse.

AMBROSE:

I wish I knew what you get out of this, Mrs. Levi.

MRS. LEVI:

That is a very proper question. I get two things: profit and pleasure.

AMBROSE:

How?

MRS. LEVI:

Mr. Kemper, I am a woman who arranges things. At present I am arranging Mr. Vandergelder's domestic affairs. Out of it I get—shall we call it: little pickings? I need little pickings, Mr. Kemper, and especially just now, when I haven't got my train fare back to New York. You see: I am frank with you.

AMBROSE:

That's your profit, Mrs. Levi; but where do you get your pleasure?

MRS. LEVI:

My pleasure? Mr. Kemper, when you artists paint a hillside or a river you change everything a little, you make thousands of little changes, don't you? Nature is never completely satisfactory and must be corrected. Well, I'm like you artists. Life as it is is never quite interesting enough for me—I'm bored, Mr. Kemper, with life as it is—and so I do things. I put my hand in here, and I put my hand in there, and I watch and I listen—and often I'm very much amused.

AMBROSE:

Rises.

Not in my affairs, Mrs. Levi.

MRS. LEVI:

Wait, I haven't finished. There's another thing. I'm very interested in this household here—in Mr. Vandergelder and all that idle, frozen money of his. I don't like the thought of it lying in great piles, useless, motionless, in the bank, Mr. Kemper. Money should circulate like rain water. It should be flowing down among the people, through dressmakers and restaurants and cabmen, setting up a little business here, and furnishing a good time there. Do you see what I mean?

AMBROSE:

Yes, I do.

MRS. LEVI:

New York should be a very happy city, Mr. Kemper, but it isn't. My late husband came from Vienna; now there's a city that understands this. I want New York to be more like Vienna and less like a collection of nervous and tired ants. And if you and Ermengarde get a good deal of Mr. Vandergelder's money, I want you to see that it starts flowing in and around a lot of people's lives. And for that reason I want you to come with me to the Harmonia Gardens Restaurant tonight.

Enter ERMENGARDE.

ERMENGARDE:

Mrs. Levi, Uncle Horace is coming.

MRS. LEVI:

Mr. Kemper, I think you'd better be going. . . .

AMBROSE *crosses to trap door and disappears down the ladder, closing trap as he goes.*

Darling girl, Mr. Kemper and I have had a very good talk.

You'll see: Mr. Vandergelder and I will be dancing at your wedding very soon—

Enter VANDERGELDER *at back. He has now added a splendid plumed hat to his costume and is carrying a standard or small flag bearing the initials of his lodge.*

Oh, Mr. Vandergelder, how handsome you look! You take my breath away. Yes, my dear girl, I'll see you soon.

Exit ERMENGARDE *back center.*

Oh, Mr. Vandergelder, I wish Irene Molloy could see you now. But then! I don't know what's come over you lately. You seem to be growing younger every day.

VANDERGELDER:
Allowing for exaggeration, Mrs. Levi. If a man eats careful there's no reason why he should look old.

MRS. LEVI:
You never said a truer word.

VANDERGELDER:
I'll never see fifty-five again.

MRS. LEVI:
Fifty-five! Why, I can see at a glance that you're the sort that will be stamping about at a hundred—and eating five meals a day, like my Uncle Harry. At fifty-five my Uncle Harry was a mere boy. I'm a judge of hands, Mr. Vandergelder—show me your hand.

Looks at it.

Lord in heaven! What a life line!

VANDERGELDER:

Where?

MRS. LEVI:

From *here* to *here*. It runs right off your hand. I don't know where it goes. They'll have to hit you on the head with a mallet. They'll have to stifle you with a sofa pillow. You'll bury us all! However, to return to our business—Mr. Vandergelder, I suppose you've changed your mind again. I suppose you've given up all idea of getting married.

VANDERGELDER:

Complacently.

Not at all, Mrs. Levi. I have news for you.

MRS. LEVI:

News?

VANDERGELDER:

Mrs. Levi, I've practically decided to ask Mrs. Molloy to be my wife.

MRS. LEVI:

Taken aback.

You have?

VANDERGELDER:

Yes, I have.

MRS. LEVI:

Oh, you have! Well, I guess that's just about the best news I ever heard. So there's nothing more for me to do but wish you every happiness under the sun and say good-by.

Crosses as if to leave.

VANDERGELDER:
Stopping her.

Well—Mrs. Levi—Surely I thought—

MRS. LEVI:
Well, I did have a little suggestion to make—but I won't. You're going to marry Irene Molloy, and that closes the matter.

VANDERGELDER:
What suggestion was that, Mrs. Levi?

MRS. LEVI:
Well—I *had* found *another* girl for you.

VANDERGELDER:
Another?

MRS. LEVI:
The most wonderful girl, the ideal wife.

VANDERGELDER:
Another, eh? What's her name?

MRS. LEVI:
Her name?

VANDERGELDER:
Yes!

MRS. LEVI:
Groping for it.

Err . . . er . . . her *name?*—Ernestina—Simple. *Miss* Ernestina Simple. But now of course all that's too late. After all, you're engaged—you're practically engaged to marry Irene Molloy.

VANDERGELDER:

Oh, I ain't engaged to Mrs. Molloy!

MRS. LEVI:

Nonsense! You can't break poor Irene's heart now and change to another girl . . . When a man at your time of life calls four times on an attractive widow like that—and sends her a pot of geraniums—that's practically an engagement!

VANDERGELDER:

That ain't an engagement!

MRS. LEVI:

And yet—! If only you were free! I've found this treasure of a girl. Every moment I felt like a traitor to Irene Molloy—but let me tell you: I couldn't help it. I told this girl all about you, just as though you were a free man. Isn't that dreadful? The fact is: she has fallen in love with you already.

VANDERGELDER:

Ernestina?

MRS. LEVI:

Ernestina Simple.

VANDERGELDER:

Ernestina Simple.

MRS. LEVI:

Of course she's a very different idea from Mrs. Molloy, Ernestina is. Like her name—simple, domestic, practical.

VANDERGELDER:

Can she cook?

MRS. LEVI:

Cook, Mr. Vandergelder? I've had two meals from her hands, and—as I live—I don't know what I've done that God should reward me with such meals.

[The following passage—adapted from a scene in Molière's L'Avare—has been cut in recent performances:

MRS. LEVI:
Continues.

Her duck! Her steak!

VANDERGELDER:

Eh! Eh! In this house we don't eat duck and steak every day, Mrs. Levi.

MRS. LEVI:

But didn't I tell you?—that's the wonderful part about it. Her duck—what was it? Pigeon! I'm alive to tell you. I don't know how she does it. It's a secret that's come down in her family. The greatest chefs would give their right hands to know it. And the steaks? Shoulder of beef—four cents a pound. Dogs wouldn't eat. But when Ernestina passes her hands over it—!!

VANDERGELDER:

Allowing for exaggeration, Mrs. Levi.

MRS. LEVI:

No exaggeration.]

I'm the best cook in the world myself, and I *know* what's good.

VANDERGELDER:

Hm. How old is she, Mrs. Levi?

MRS. LEVI:

Nineteen, well—say twenty.

VANDERGELDER:

Twenty, Mrs. Levi? Girls of twenty are apt to favor young fellows of their own age.

MRS. LEVI:

But you don't listen to me. And you don't know the girl. Mr. Vandergelder, she has a positive horror of flighty, brainless young men. A fine head of gray hair, she says, is worth twenty shined up with goose grease. No, sir. "I like a man that's *settled*"—in so many words she said it.

VANDERGELDER:

That's . . . that's not usual, Mrs. Levi.

MRS. LEVI:

Usual? I'm not wearing myself to the bone hunting up *usual* girls to interest you, Mr. Vandergelder. Usual, indeed. Listen to me. Do you know the sort of pictures she has on her wall? Is it any of these young Romeos and Lochinvars? No!—it's Moses on the Mountain—that's what she's got. If you want to make her happy, you give her a picture of Methuselah surrounded by his grandchildren. That's my advice to you.

[*The following passage—also based on Molière—has generally been cut in performance:*

VANDERGELDER:

I hope . . . hm . . . that she has some means, Mrs. Levi. I have a large household to run.

MRS. LEVI:

Ernestina? She'll bring you five thousand dollars a year.

VANDERGELDER:

Eh! Eh!

MRS. LEVI:

Listen to me, Mr. Vandergelder. You're a man of sense, I hope. A man that can reckon. In the first place, she's an orphan. She's been brought up with a great saving of food. What does she eat herself? Apples and lettuce. It's what she's been used to eat and what she likes best. She saves you two thousand a year right there. Secondly, she makes her own clothes—out of old table-cloths and window curtains. And she's the best-dressed woman in Brooklyn this minute. She saves you a thousand dollars right there. Thirdly, her health is of iron—

VANDERGELDER:

But, Mrs. Levi, that's not money in the pocket.

MRS. LEVI:

We're talking about marriage, aren't we, Mr. Vandergelder? The money she saves while she's in Brooklyn is none of your affair—but if she were your wife that would be *money.* Yes, sir, that's money.]

VANDERGELDER:

What's her family?

MRS. LEVI:

Her father?—God be good to him! He was the best—what am I trying to say?—the best undertaker in Brooklyn, respected, esteemed. He knew all the best people—knew them well, even before they died. So—well, that's the way it is.

Lowering her voice, intimately.

Now let me tell you a little more of her appearance. Can you

hear me: as I say, a beautiful girl, beautiful, I've seen her go
down the street—you know what I mean?—the young men
get dizzy. They have to lean against lampposts. And she?
Modest, eyes on the ground—I'm not going to tell you any
more. . . . Couldn't you come to New York today?

VANDERGELDER:

I was thinking of coming to New York this afternoon. . . .

MRS. LEVI:

You were? Well now, I wonder if something could be
arranged—oh, she's so eager to see you! Let me see . . .

VANDERGELDER:

Could I . . . Mrs. Levi, could I give you a little dinner,
maybe?

MRS. LEVI:

Really, come to think of it, I don't see where I could get the
time. I'm so busy over that wretched lawsuit of mine. Yes. If
I win it, I don't mind telling you, I'll be what's called a very
rich woman. I'll own half of Long Island, that's a fact. But
just now I'm at my wit's end for a little help, just enough
money to finish it off. My wit's end!

She looks in her handbag.

In order not to hear this, VANDERGELDER *has a series of
coughs, sneezes and minor convulsions.*

But perhaps I could arrange a little dinner; I'll see. Yes, for
that lawsuit all I need is fifty dollars, and Staten Island's as
good as mine. I've been trotting all over New York for you,
trying to find you a suitable wife.

VANDERGELDER:

Fifty dollars!!

MRS. LEVI:

Two whole months I've been . . .

VANDERGELDER:

Fifty dollars, Mrs. Levi . . . is no joke.

Producing purse.

I don't know where money's gone to these days. It's in hiding. . . . There's twenty . . . well, there's twenty-five. I can't spare no more, not now I can't.

MRS. LEVI:

Well, this will help—will help somewhat. Now let me tell you what we'll do. I'll bring Ernestina to that restaurant on the Battery. You know it: the Harmonia Gardens. It's good, but it's not flashy. Now, Mr. Vandergelder, I think it'd be nice if just this once you'd order a real nice dinner. I guess you can afford it.

VANDERGELDER:

Well, just this once.

MRS. LEVI:

A chicken wouldn't hurt.

VANDERGELDER:

Chicken!!—Well, just this once.

MRS. LEVI:

And a little wine.

VANDERGELDER:

Wine? Well, just this once.

MRS. LEVI:

Now about Mrs. Molloy—what do you think? Shall we call that subject closed?

VANDERGELDER:

No, not at all, Mrs. Levi, I want to have dinner with Miss . . . with Miss . . .

MRS. LEVI:

Simple.

VANDERGELDER:

With Miss Simple; but first I want to make another call on Mrs. Molloy.

MRS. LEVI:

Dear, dear, dear! And Miss Simple? What races you make me run! Very well; I'll meet you on one of those benches in front of Mrs. Molloy's hat store at four thirty, as usual.

Trap door rises, and CORNELIUS' *head appears.*

CORNELIUS:

The buggy's here, ready for the parade, Mr. Vandergelder.

VANDERGELDER:

Call Barnaby. I want to talk to both of you.

CORNELIUS:

Yes, Mr. Vandergelder.

Exit CORNELIUS *down trap door. Leaves trap open.*

MRS. LEVI:
Now do put your thoughts in order, Mr. Vandergelder. I can't keep upsetting and disturbing the finest women in New York City unless you mean business.

VANDERGELDER:
Oh, I mean business all right!

MRS. LEVI:
I hope so. Because, you know, you're playing a very dangerous game.

VANDERGELDER:
Dangerous?—Dangerous, Mrs. Levi?

MRS. LEVI:
Of course, it's dangerous—and there's a name for it! You're tampering with these women's affections, aren't you? And the only way you can save yourself now is to be married to *someone* by the end of next week. So think that over!

Exit center back.

Enter CORNELIUS *and* BARNABY, *by the trap door.*

VANDERGELDER:
This morning I'm joining my lodge parade, and this afternoon I'm going to New York. When I come back, there are going to be some changes in the house here. I'll tell you what the change is, but I don't want you discussing it amongst yourselves: you're going to have a mistress.

BARNABY:
Seventeen; round-faced, wide-eyed innocence; wearing a green apron.

I'm too young, Mr. Vandergelder!!

VANDERGELDER:

Not yours! Death and damnation! Not yours, idiot—*mine!*

Then, realizing:

Hey! Hold your tongue until you're spoken to! I'm thinking of getting married.

CORNELIUS:

Crosses, hand outstretched.

Many congratulations, Mr. Vandergelder, and my compliments to the lady.

VANDERGELDER:

That's none of your business. Now go back to the store.

The BOYS *start down the ladder,* BARNABY *first.*

Have you got any questions you want to ask before I go?

CORNELIUS:

Mr. Vandergelder—er—Mr. Vandergelder, does the chief clerk get one evening off every week?

VANDERGELDER:

So that's the way you begin being chief clerk, is it? When I was your age I got up at five; I didn't close the shop until ten at night, and then I put in a good hour at the account books. The world's going to pieces. You elegant ladies lie in bed until six and at nine o'clock at night you rush to close the door so fast the line of customers bark their noses. No, sir—you'll attend to the store as usual, and on Friday and Saturday nights you'll remain open until ten—now hear what I say! This is the first time I've been away from the store overnight. When I come back I want to hear that you've run the place perfectly in my absence. If I hear of any foolishness, I'll discharge you. An evening free! Do you suppose that *I* had evenings free?

At the top of his complacency.

If I'd had evenings free I wouldn't be what I am now!

He marches out, right.

BARNABY:
Watching him go.

The horses nearly ran away when they saw him. What's the matter, Cornelius?

CORNELIUS:
Sits in dejected thought.

Chief clerk! Promoted from chief clerk to chief clerk.

BARNABY:
Don't you like it?

CORNELIUS:
Chief clerk!—and if I'm good, in ten years I'll be promoted to chief clerk again. Thirty-three years old and I still don't get an evening free? When am I going to begin to live?

BARNABY:
Well—ah . . . you can begin to live on Sundays, Cornelius.

CORNELIUS:
That's not living. Twice to church, and old Wolf-trap's eyes on the back of my head the whole time. And as for holidays! What did we do last Christmas? All those canned tomatoes went bad

and exploded. We had to clean up the mess all afternoon. Was that living?

BARNABY:

Holding his nose at the memory of the bad smell.

No!!!

CORNELIUS:

Rising with sudden resolution.

Barnaby, how much money have you got—where you can get at it?

BARNABY:

Oh—three dollars. Why, Cornelius?

CORNELIUS:

You and I are going to New York.

BARNABY:

Cornelius!!! We can't! Close the store?

CORNELIUS:

Some more rotten-tomato cans are going to explode.

BARNABY:

Holy cabooses! How do you know?

CORNELIUS:

I know they're rotten. All you have to do is to light a match under them. They'll make such a smell that customers can't come into the place for twenty-four hours. That'll get us an evening free. We're going to New York too, Barnaby, we're going to live! I'm going to have enough adventures to last me until I'm *partner.* So go and get your Sunday clothes on.

BARNABY:

Wha-a-a-t?

CORNELIUS:

Yes, I mean it. We're going to have a good meal; and we're going to be in danger; and we're going to get almost arrested; and we're going to spend all our money.

BARNABY:

Holy cabooses!!

CORNELIUS:

And one more thing: we're not coming back to Yonkers until we've kissed a girl.

BARNABY:

Kissed a girl! Cornelius, you can't do that. You don't know any girls.

CORNELIUS:

I'm thirty-three. I've got to begin sometime.

BARNABY:

I'm only seventeen, Cornelius. It isn't so urgent for me.

CORNELIUS:

Don't start backing down now—if the worst comes to the worst and we get discharged from here we can always join the Army.

BARNABY:

Uh—did I hear you say that you'd be old Wolf-trap's partner?

CORNELIUS:

How can I help it? He's growing old. If you go to bed at nine and open the store at six, you get promoted upward whether you like it or not.

BARNABY:

My! Partner.

CORNELIUS:

Oh, there's no way of getting away from it. You and I will be Vandergelders.

BARNABY:

I? Oh, no—I may rise a little, but I'll never be a Vandergelder.

CORNELIUS:

Listen—everybody thinks when he gets rich he'll be a different kind of rich person from the rich people he sees around him; later on he finds out there's only one kind of rich person, and he's it.

BARNABY:

Oh, but I'll—

CORNELIUS:

No. The best of all would be a person who has all the good things a poor person has, and all the good meals a rich person has, but that's never been known. No, you and I are going to be Vandergelders; all the more reason, then, for us to try and get some living and some adventure into us now—will you come, Barnaby?

BARNABY:

In a struggle with his fears, a whirlwind of words.

But Wolf-trap—KRR-pt, Gertrude-KRR-pt—

With a sudden cry of agreement.

Yes, Cornelius!

Enter MRS. LEVI, ERMENGARDE *and* GERTRUDE *from back center. The* BOYS *start down the ladder,* CORNELIUS *last.*

MRS. LEVI:

Mr. Hackl, is the trunk waiting at the station?

CORNELIUS:

Yes, Mrs. Levi.

Closes the trap door.

MRS. LEVI:

Take a last look, Ermengarde.

ERMENGARDE:

What?

MRS. LEVI:

Take a last look at your girlhood home, dear. I remember when I left my home. I gave a whinny like a young colt, and off I went.

ERMENGARDE *and* GERTRUDE *exit.*

ERMENGARDE:

As they go.

Oh, Gertrude, do you think I ought to get married this way? A young girl has to be so careful!

MRS. LEVI *is alone. She addresses the audience.*

MRS. LEVI:

You know, I think I'm going to have this room with *blue* wallpaper,—yes, in blue!

Hurries out after the others.

BARNABY *comes up trap door, looks off right, then lies on floor, gazing down through the trap door.*

BARNABY:

All clear up here, Cornelius! Cornelius—hold the candle steady a minute—the bottom row's all right—but try the top now . . . they're swelled up like they are ready to bust!

BANG.

Holy CABOOSES!

BANG, BANG.

Cornelius! I can smell it up here!

Rises and dances about, holding his nose.

CORNELIUS:
Rushing up the trap door.

Get into your Sunday clothes, Barnaby. We're going to New York!

As they run out . . . there is a big explosion. A shower of tomato cans comes up from below, as—

THE
CURTAIN
FALLS

Act II

Mrs. Molloy's hat shop, New York City.

There are two entrances. One door at the extreme right of the back wall, to Mrs. Molloy's workroom; one at the back left corner, to the street. The whole left wall is taken up with the show windows, filled with hats. It is separated from the shop by a low brass rail, hung with net; during the act both MRS. MOLLOY and BARNABY stoop under the rail and go into the shop window. By the street door stands a large cheval glass. In the middle of the back wall is a large wardrobe or clothes cupboard, filled with ladies' coats, large enough for CORNELIUS to hide in. At the left, beginning at the back wall, between the wardrobe and the workroom door, a long counter extends toward the audience, almost to the footlights. In the center of the room is a large round table with a low-hanging red cloth. There are a small gilt chair by the wardrobe and two chairs in front of the counter. Over the street door and the workroom door are bells which ring when the doors are opened.

As the curtain rises, MRS. MOLLOY is in the window, standing on a box, reaching up to put hats on the stand. MINNIE FAY *is sewing by the counter.* MRS. MOLLOY *has a pair of felt over-shoes, to be removed later.*

MRS. MOLLOY:

Minnie, you're a fool. Of course I shall marry Horace Van-dergelder.

MINNIE:

Oh, Mrs. Molloy! I didn't ask you. I wouldn't dream of ask-ing you such a personal question.

MRS. MOLLOY:

Well, it's what you meant, isn't it? And there's your answer. I shall certainly marry Horace Vandergelder if he asks me.

Crawls under window rail, into the room, singing loudly.

MINNIE:

I know it's none of my business . . .

MRS. MOLLOY:

Speak up, Minnie, I can't hear you.

MINNIE:

. . . but do you . . . do you . . . ?

MRS. MOLLOY:

Having crossed the room, is busy at the counter.

Minnie, you're a fool. Say it: Do I love him? Of course, I don't love him. But I have two good reasons for marrying him just the same. Minnie, put something on that hat. It's not ugly enough.

Throws hat over counter.

MINNIE:

Catching and taking hat to table.

Not ugly enough!

MRS. MOLLOY:

I couldn't sell it. Put a . . . put a sponge on it.

MINNIE:

Why, Mrs. Molloy, you're in such a *mood* today.

MRS. MOLLOY:

In the first place I shall marry Mr. Vandergelder to get away from the millinery business. I've hated it from the first day I had anything to do with it. Minnie, I hate hats.

Sings loudly again.

MINNIE:

Why, what's the matter with the millinery business?

MRS. MOLLOY:

Crossing to window with two hats.

I can no longer stand being suspected of being a wicked woman, while I have nothing to show for it. I can't stand it.

She crawls under rail into window.

MINNIE:

Why, no one would dream of suspecting you—

MRS. MOLLOY:

On her knees, she looks over the rail.

Minnie, you're a fool. All millineresses are suspected of being wicked women. Why, half the time all those women come into the shop merely to look at me.

MINNIE:

Oh!

MRS. MOLLOY:

They enjoy the suspicion. But they aren't certain. If they were *certain* I was a wicked woman, they wouldn't put foot in this place again. Do I go to restaurants? No, it would be bad for business. Do I go to balls, or theaters, or operas? No, it would be bad for business. The only men I ever meet are feather merchants.

Crawls out of window, but gazes intently into the street.

What are those two young men doing out there on that park bench? Take my word for it, Minnie, either I marry Horace Vandergelder, or I break out of this place like a fire engine. I'll go to every theater and ball and opera in New York City.

Returns to counter, singing again.

MINNIE:

But Mr. Vandergelder's not . . . .

MRS. MOLLOY:

Speak up, Minnie, I can't hear you.

MINNIE:

. . . I don't think he's attractive.

MRS. MOLLOY:

But what I think he is—and it's very important—I think he'd make a good fighter.

MINNIE:

Mrs. Molloy!

MRS. MOLLOY:

Take my word for it, Minnie: the best part of married life is the fights. The rest is merely so-so.

MINNIE:
Fingers in ears.

I won't listen.

MRS. MOLLOY:

Peter Molloy—God rest him!—was a fine arguing man. I pity the woman whose husband slams the door and walks out of the house at the beginning of an argument. Peter Molloy would stand up and fight for hours on end. He'd even throw things, Minnie, and there's no pleasure to equal that. When I felt tired I'd start a good bloodwarming fight and it'd take ten years off my age; now Horace Vandergelder would put up a good fight; I know it. I've a mind to marry him.

MINNIE:

I think they're just awful, the things you're saying today.

MRS. MOLLOY:

Well, I'm enjoying them myself, too.

MINNIE:
At the window.

Mrs. Molloy, those two men out in the street—

MRS. MOLLOY:

What?

MINNIE:

Those men. It looks as if they meant to come in here.

MRS. MOLLOY:

Well now, it's time some men came into this place. I give you the younger one, Minnie.

MINNIE:

Aren't you terrible!

MRS. MOLLOY *sits on center table, while* MINNIE *takes off her felt overshoes.*

MRS. MOLLOY:

Wait till I get my hands on that older one! Mark my words, Minnie, we'll get an adventure out of this yet. Adventure, adventure! Why does everybody have adventures except me, Minnie? Because I have no spirit, I have no gumption. Minnie, they're coming in here. Let's go into the workroom and make them wait for us for a minute.

MINNIE:

Oh, but Mrs. Molloy . . . my work!. . .

MRS. MOLLOY:

Running to workroom.

Hurry up, be quick now, Minnie!

They go out to workroom.

BARNABY *and* CORNELIUS *run in from street, leaving front door open. They are dressed in the stiff discomfort of their Sunday clothes.* CORNELIUS *wears a bowler hat,* BARNABY *a straw hat too large for him.*

BARNABY:

No one's here.

CORNELIUS:

Some women were here a minute ago. I saw them.

They jump back to the street door and peer down the street.

That's Wolf-trap all right!

Coming back.

Well, we've got to hide here until he passes by.

BARNABY:

He's sitting down on that bench. It may be quite a while.

CORNELIUS:

When these women come in, we'll have to make conversation until he's gone away. We'll pretend we're buying a hat. How much money have you got now?

BARNABY:

Counting his money.

Forty cents for the train—seventy cents for dinner—twenty cents to see the whale—and a dollar I lost—I have seventy cents.

CORNELIUS:

And I have a dollar seventy-five. I wish I knew how much hats cost!

BARNABY:

Is this an adventure, Cornelius?

CORNELIUS:

No, but it may be.

BARNABY:

I think it is. There we wander around New York all day and nothing happens; and then we come to the quietest street in the whole city and suddenly Mr. Vandergelder turns the corner.

Going to door.

I think that's an adventure. I think . . . Cornelius! That Mrs. Levi is there now. She's sitting down on the bench with him.

CORNELIUS:

What do you know about that! We know only one person in all New York City, and there she is!

BARNABY:

Even if our adventure came along now I'd be too tired to enjoy it. Cornelius, why isn't this an adventure?

CORNELIUS:

Don't be asking that. When you're in an adventure, you'll know it all right.

BARNABY:

Maybe I wouldn't. Cornelius, let's arrange a signal for you to give me when an adventure's really going on. For instance, Cornelius, you say . . . uh . . . uh . . . *pudding;* you say *pudding* to me if it's an adventure we're in.

CORNELIUS:

I wonder where the lady who runs this store is? What's her name again?

BARNABY:

"Mrs. Molloy, hats for ladies."

CORNELIUS:

Oh yes. I must think over what I'm going to say when she comes in.

To counter.

"Good afternoon, Mrs. Molloy, wonderful weather we're having. We've been looking everywhere for some beautiful hats."

BARNABY:

That's fine, Cornelius!

CORNELIUS:

"Good afternoon, Mrs. Molloy; wonderful weather . . . " We'll make her think we're very rich.

One hand in trouser pocket, the other on back of chair.

"Good afternoon, Mrs. Molloy . . . " You keep one eye on the door the whole time. "We've been looking everywhere for . . . "

Enter MRS. MOLLOY *from the workroom.*

MRS. MOLLOY:

Behind the counter.

Oh, I'm sorry. Have I kept you waiting? Good afternoon, gentlemen.

CORNELIUS:

Hat off.

Here, Cornelius Hackl.

BARNABY:

Hat off.

Here, Barnaby Tucker.

MRS. MOLLOY:

I'm very happy to meet you. Perhaps I can help you. Won't you sit down?

CORNELIUS:

Thank you, we will.

The BOYS *place their hats on the table, then sit down at the counter facing Mrs. Molloy.*

You see, Mrs. Molloy, we're looking for hats. We've looked everywhere. Do you know what we heard? Go to Mrs. Molloy's, they said. So we came here. Only place we *could* go . . .

MRS. MOLLOY:

Well now, that's *very* complimentary.

CORNELIUS:

. . . and we were right. Everybody was right.

MRS. MOLLOY:

You wish to choose some hats for a friend?

CORNELIUS:

Yes, exactly.

Kicks Barnaby.

BARNABY:

Yes, exactly.

CORNELIUS:

We were thinking of five or six, weren't we, Barnaby?

BARNABY:

Er-five.

CORNELIUS:

You see, Mrs. Molloy, money's no object with us. None at all.

MRS. MOLLOY:

Why, Mr. Hackl . . .

CORNELIUS:

Rises and goes toward street door.

. . . I beg your pardon, what an interesting street! Something happening every minute. Passers-by, and . . .

BARNABY *runs to join him.*

MRS. MOLLOY:

You're from out of town, Mr. Hackl?

CORNELIUS:

Coming back.

Yes, ma'am—Barnaby, just keep your eye on the street, will you? You won't see that in Yonkers every day.

BARNABY *remains kneeling at street door.*

BARNABY:

Oh yes, I will.

CORNELIUS:

Not all of it.

MRS. MOLLOY:

Now this friend of yours—couldn't she come in with you someday and choose her hats herself?

CORNELIUS:

Sits at counter.

No. Oh, no. It's a surprise for her.

MRS. MOLLOY:

Indeed? That may be a little difficult, Mr. Hackl. It's not entirely customary.—Your friend's very interested in the street, Mr. Hackl.

CORNELIUS:

Oh yes. Yes. He has reason to be.

MRS. MOLLOY:

You said you were from out of town?

CORNELIUS:

Yes, we're from Yonkers.

MRS. MOLLOY:

Yonkers?

CORNELIUS:

Yonkers . . . yes, Yonkers.

He gazes rapt into her eyes.

You should know Yonkers, Mrs. Molloy. Hudson River; Palisades; drives; some say it's the most beautiful town in the world; that's what they say.

MRS. MOLLOY:

Is that so!

CORNELIUS:

Rises.

Mrs. Molloy, if you ever had a Sunday free, I'd . . . we'd like to show you Yonkers. Y'know, it's very historic, too.

MRS. MOLLOY:

That's very kind of you. Well, perhaps . . . now about those hats.

Takes two hats from under counter, and crosses to back center of the room.

CORNELIUS:

Following.

Is there . . . Have you a . . . Maybe Mr. Molloy would like to see Yonkers too?

MRS. MOLLOY:

Oh, I'm a widow, Mr. Hackl.

CORNELIUS:

Joyfully.

You are!

With sudden gravity.

Oh, that's too bad. Mr. Molloy would have enjoyed Yonkers.

MRS. MOLLOY:

Very likely. Now about these hats. Is your friend dark or light?

CORNELIUS:

Don't think about that for a minute. Any hat you'd like would be perfectly all right with her.

MRS. MOLLOY:

Really!

She puts one on.

Do you like this one?

CORNELIUS:

In awe-struck admiration.

Barnaby!

In sudden anger.

Barnaby! Look!

BARNABY *turns; unimpressed, he laughs vaguely, and turns to door again.*

Mrs. Molloy, that's the most beautiful hat I ever saw.

BARNABY *now crawls under the rail into the window.*

MRS. MOLLOY:

Your friend is acting very strangely, Mr. Hackl.

CORNELIUS:

Barnaby, stop acting strangely. When the street's quiet and empty, come back and talk to us. What was I saying? Oh yes: Mrs. Molloy, you should know Yonkers.

MRS. MOLLOY:

Hat off.

The fact is, I have a friend in Yonkers. Perhaps you know him. It's always so foolish to ask in cases like that, isn't it?

They both laugh over this with increasing congeniality.

MRS. MOLLOY *goes to counter with hats from table.*
CORNELIUS *follows.*

It's a Mr. Vandergelder.

CORNELIUS:
Stops abruptly.

What was that you said?

MRS. MOLLOY:
Then you do know him?

CORNELIUS:
Horace Vandergelder?

MRS. MOLLOY:
Yes, that's right.

CORNELIUS:
Know him!

Look to Barnaby.

Why, no. No!

BARNABY:
No! No!

CORNELIUS:
Starting to glide about the room, in search of a hiding place.

I beg your pardon, Mrs. Molloy—what an attractive shop you have!

Smiling fixedly at her he moves to the workshop door.

And where does this door lead to?

Opens it, and is alarmed by the bell which rings above it.

MRS. MOLLOY:

Why, Mr. Hackl, that's my workroom.

CORNELIUS:

Everything here is so interesting.

Looks under counter.

Every corner. Every door, Mrs. Molloy. Barnaby, notice the interesting doors and cupboards.

He opens the cupboard door.

Deeply interesting. Coats for ladies.

Laughs.

Barnaby, make a note of the table. Precious piece of furniture, with a low-hanging cloth, I see.

Stretches his leg under table.

MRS. MOLLOY:

Taking a hat from box left of wardrobe.

Perhaps your friend might like some of this new Italian straw. Mr. Vandergelder's a substantial man and very well liked, they tell me.

CORNELIUS:

A lovely man, Mrs. Molloy.

MRS. MOLLOY:

Oh yes—charming, charming!

CORNELIUS:

Smiling sweetly.

Has only one fault, as far as I know; he's hard as nails; but apart from that, as you say, a charming nature, ma'am.

MRS. MOLLOY:

And a large circle of friends—?

CORNELIUS:

Yes, indeed, yes indeed—five or six.

BARNABY:

Five!

CORNELIUS:

He comes and calls on you here from time to time, I suppose.

MRS. MOLLOY:

Turns from mirror where she has been putting a hat on.

This summer we'll be wearing ribbons down our back. Yes, as a matter of fact I am expecting a call from him this afternoon.

Hat off.

BARNABY:

I think . . . Cornelius! I think . . . !!

MRS. MOLLOY:

Now to show you some more hats—

BARNABY:

Look out!

He takes a flying leap over the rail and flings himself under the table.

CORNELIUS:

Begging your pardon, Mrs. Molloy.

He jumps into the cupboard.

MRS. MOLLOY:

Gentlemen! Mr. Hackl! Come right out of there this minute!

CORNELIUS:

Sticking his head out of the wardrobe door.

Help us just this once, Mrs. Molloy! We'll explain later!

MRS. MOLLOY:

Mr. Hackl!

BARNABY:

We're as innocent as can be, Mrs. Molloy.

MRS. MOLLOY:

But really! Gentlemen! I can't have this! *What are you doing?*

BARNABY:

Cornelius! Cornelius! Pudding?

CORNELIUS:

A shout.

Pudding!

They disappear. Enter from the street MRS. LEVI, *followed by* MR. VANDERGELDER. VANDERGELDER *is dressed in a too-bright checked suit, and wears a green derby—or bowler—hat. He is carrying a large ornate box of chocolates in one hand, and a cane in the other.*

MRS. LEVI:

Irene, my darling child, how *are* you? Heaven be good to us, how well you look!

They kiss.

MRS. MOLLOY:

But what a surprise! And Mr. Vandergelder in New York—what a pleasure!

VANDERGELDER:

Swaying back and forth on his heels complacently.

Good afternoon, Mrs. Molloy.

They shake hands. MRS. MOLLOY *brings chair from counter for him. He sits at left of table.*

MRS. LEVI:

Yes, Mr. Vandergelder's in New York. Yonkers lies up there— *decimated* today. Irene, we thought we'd pay you a very short call. Now you'll tell us if it's inconvenient, won't you?

MRS. MOLLOY:

Placing a chair for Mrs. Levi at right of table.

Inconvenient, Dolly! The idea! Why, it's sweet of you to come.

She notices the boys' hats on the table—sticks a spray of flowers into crown of Cornelius' bowler and winds a piece of chiffon round Barnaby's panama.

VANDERGELDER:

We waited outside a moment.

MRS. LEVI:

Mr. Vandergelder thought he saw two customers coming in—two men.

MRS. MOLLOY:

Men! Men, Mr. Vandergelder? Why, what will you be saying next?

MRS. LEVI:

Then we'll sit down for a minute or two. . . .

MRS. MOLLOY:

Wishing to get them out of the shop into the workroom.

Before you sit down—

She pushes them both.

Before you sit down, there's something I want to show you. I want to show Mr. Vandergelder my workroom, too.

MRS. LEVI:

I've seen the workroom a hundred times. I'll stay right here and try on some of these hats.

MRS. MOLLOY:

No, Dolly, you come too. I have something for you. Come along, everybody.

Exit MRS. LEVI *to workroom.*

Mr. Vandergelder, I want your advice. You don't know how helpless a woman in business is. Oh, I feel I need advice every minute from a fine business head like yours.

Exit VANDERGELDER *to workroom.* MRS. MOLLOY *shouts this line and then slams the workroom door.*

Now I shut the door!!

Exit MRS. MOLLOY.

CORNELIUS *puts his head out of the wardrobe door and gradually comes out into the room, leaving door open.*

CORNELIUS:

Hsst!

BARNABY:

Pokes his head out from under the table.

Maybe she wants us to go, Cornelius?

CORNELIUS:

Certainly I won't go. Mrs. Molloy would think we were just thoughtless fellows. No, all I want is to stretch a minute.

BARNABY:

What are you going to do when he's gone, Cornelius? Are we just going to run away?

CORNELIUS:

Well . . . I don't know yet. I like Mrs. Molloy a lot. I wouldn't like her to think badly of me. I think I'll buy a hat. We can walk home to Yonkers, even if it takes us all night. I wonder how much hats cost. Barnaby, give me all the money you've got.

As he leans over to take the money, he sneezes. Both return to their hiding places in alarm; then emerge again.

My, all those perfumes in that cupboard tickle my nose! But I like it in there . . . it's a woman's world, and very different.

BARNABY:

I like it where I am, too; only I'd like it better if I had a pillow.

CORNELIUS:

Taking coat from wardrobe.

Here, take one of these coats. I'll roll it up for you so it won't get mussed. Ladies don't like to have their coats mussed.

BARNABY:

That's fine. Now I can just lie here and hear Mr. Vandergelder talk.

CORNELIUS *goes slowly above table towards cheval mirror, repeating Mrs. Molloy's line dreamily:*

CORNELIUS:

This summer we'll be wearing ribbons down our back. . . .

BARNABY:

Can I take off my shoes, Cornelius?

CORNELIUS *does not reply. He comes to the footlights and addresses the audience, in completely simple naïve sincerity:*

CORNELIUS:

Isn't the world full of wonderful things. There we sit cooped up in Yonkers for years and years and all the time wonderful people like Mrs. Molloy are walking around in New York and we don't know them at all. I don't know whether—from where you're sitting—you can see—well, for instance, the way

He points to the edge of his right eye.

her eye and forehead and cheek come together, up here. Can you? And the kind of fireworks that shoot out of her eyes all the time. I tell you right now: a fine woman is the greatest work of God. You can talk all you like about Niagara Falls and the Pyramids; they aren't in it at all. Of course, up there at Yonkers they came into the store all the time, and bought this and that, and I said, "Yes, ma'am," and "That'll be seventy-five cents, ma'am"; and I *watched* them. But today I've talked to one, equal to equal, equal to equal, and to the finest one that ever existed, in my opinion. They're so different from men! Everything that they say and do is so different that you feel like laughing all the time.

He laughs.

Golly, they're different from men. And they're awfully mysterious, too. You never can be really sure what's going on in their heads. They have a kind of wall around them all the time—of pride and a sort of play-acting: I bet you could know a woman a hundred years without ever being really sure whether she liked you or not. This minute I'm in danger. I'm in danger of losing my job and my future and everything that people think is important; but I don't care. Even if I have to dig ditches for the rest of my life, I'll be a ditch digger who once had a wonderful day.

Barnaby!

BARNABY:
Oh, you woke me up!

CORNELIUS:
Kneels.

Barnaby, we can't go back to Yonkers yet and you know why.

BARNABY:

Why not?

CORNELIUS:

We've had a good meal. We've had an adventure. We've been in danger of getting arrested. There's only one more thing we've got to do before we go back to be successes in Yonkers.

BARNABY:

Cornelius! You're never going to kiss Mrs. Molloy!

CORNELIUS:

Maybe.

BARNABY:

But she'll scream.

CORNELIUS:

Barnaby, you don't know anything at all. You might as well know right now that everybody except us goes through life kissing right and left all the time.

BARNABY:

Pauses for reflection: humbly:

Well, thanks for telling me, Cornelius. I often wondered.

Enter MRS. LEVI *from workroom.*

MRS. LEVI:

Just a minute, Irene. I must find my handkerchief.

CORNELIUS, *caught by the arrival of Mrs. Levi, drops to his hands and knees, and starts very slowly to crawl back to the wardrobe, as though the slowness rendered him invisible.* MRS. LEVI, *leaning over the counter, watches him. From the cupboard he puts his head out of it and looks pleadingly at her.*

Why, Mr. Hackl, I thought you were up in Yonkers.

CORNELIUS:

I almost always am, Mrs. Levi. Oh, Mrs. Levi, don't tell Mr. Vandergelder! I'll explain everything later.

BARNABY:

Puts head out.

We're terribly innocent, Mrs. Levi.

MRS. LEVI:

Why, who's that?

BARNABY:

Barnaby Tucker—just paying a call.

MRS. LEVI:

Looking under counter and even shaking out her skirts.

Well, who else is here?

CORNELIUS:

Just the two of us, Mrs. Levi, that's all.

MRS. LEVI:

Old friends of Mrs. Molloy's, is that it?

CORNELIUS:

We never knew her before a few minutes ago, but we like her a lot—don't we, Barnaby? In fact, I think she's . . . I think she's the finest person in the world. I'm ready to tell that to anybody.

MRS. LEVI:

And does she think *you're* the finest person in the world?

CORNELIUS:

Oh, no. I don't suppose she even notices that I'm alive.

MRS. LEVI:

Well, I think she must notice that you're alive in that cupboard, Mr. Hackl. Well, if I were you, I'd get back into it right away. Somebody could be coming in any minute.

CORNELIUS *disappears. She sits unconcernedly in chair right. Enter* MRS. MOLLOY.

MRS. MOLLOY:

Leaving door open and looking about in concealed alarm.

Can I help you, Dolly?

MRS. LEVI:

No, no, no. I was just blowing my nose.

Enter VANDERGELDER *from workroom.*

VANDERGELDER:

Mrs. Molloy, I've got some advice to give you about your business.

MRS. MOLLOY *comes to the center of the room and puts Barnaby's hat on floor in window, then Cornelius' hat on the counter.*

MRS. LEVI:

Oh, advice from Mr. Vandergelder! The whole city should hear this.

VANDERGELDER:

Standing in the workroom door, pompously:

In the first place, the aim of business is to make profit.

MRS. MOLLOY:

Is that so?

MRS. LEVI:

I never heard it put so clearly before. Did you hear it?

VANDERGELDER:

Crossing the room to the left.

You pay those girls of yours too much. You pay them as much as men. Girls like that enjoy their work. Wages, Mrs. Molloy, are paid to make people do work they don't want to do.

MRS. LEVI:

Mr. Vandergelder thinks so ably. And that's exactly the way his business is run up in Yonkers.

VANDERGELDER:

Patting her hand.

Mrs. Molloy, I'd like for you to come up to Yonkers.

MRS. MOLLOY:

That would be very nice.

He hands her the box of chocolates.

Oh, thank you. As a matter of fact, I know someone from Yonkers, someone else.

VANDERGELDER:

Hangs hat on the cheval mirror.

Oh? Who's that?

MRS. MOLLOY *puts chocolates on table and brings gilt chair forward and sits center at table facing the audience.*

MRS. MOLLOY:

Someone quite well-to-do, I believe, though a little free and easy in his behavior. Mr. Vandergelder, do you know Mr. Cornelius Hackl in Yonkers?

VANDERGELDER:

I know him like I know my own boot. He's my head clerk.

MRS. MOLLOY:

Is that so?

VANDERGELDER:

He's been in my store for ten years.

MRS. MOLLOY:

Well, I never!

VANDERGELDER:

Where would you have known him?

MRS. MOLLOY *is in silent confusion. She looks for help to Mrs. Levi, seated at right end of table.*

MRS. LEVI:

Groping for means to help Mrs. Molloy.

Err . . . blah . . . err . . . bl . . . er . . . Oh, just one of those chance meetings, I suppose.

MRS. MOLLOY:

Yes, oh yes! One of those chance meetings.

VANDERGELDER:

What? Chance meetings? Cornelius Hackl has no right to chance meetings. Where was it?

MRS. MOLLOY:

Really, Mr. Vandergelder, it's very unlike you to question me in such a way. I think Mr. Hackl is better known than you think he is.

VANDERGELDER:

Nonsense.

MRS. MOLLOY:

He's in New York often, and he's very well liked.

MRS. LEVI:

Having found her idea, with decision.

Well, the truth might as well come out now as later. Mr. Vandergelder, Irene is quite right. Your head clerk is often in New York. Goes everywhere; has an army of friends. Everybody knows Cornelius Hackl.

VANDERGELDER:

Laughs blandly and sits in chair at left of table.

He never comes to New York. He works all day in my store and at nine o'clock at night he goes to sleep in the bran room.

MRS. LEVI:

So you think. But it's not true.

VANDERGELDER:

Dolly Gallagher, you're crazy.

MRS. LEVI:

Listen to me. You keep your nose so deep in your account books you don't know what goes on. Yes, by day, Cornelius Hackl is your faithful trusted clerk—that's true; but by night!

Well, he leads a double life, that's all! He's here at the opera; at the great restaurants; in all the fashionable homes . . . why, he's at the Harmonia Gardens Restaurant three nights a week. The fact is, he's the wittiest, gayest, naughtiest, most delightful man in New York. Well, he's just *the* famous Cornelius Hackl!

VANDERGELDER:
Sure of himself.

It ain't the same man. If I ever thought Cornelius Hackl came to New York, I'd discharge him.

MRS. LEVI:
Who took the horses out of Jenny Lind's carriage and pulled her through the streets?

MRS. MOLLOY:
Who?

MRS. LEVI:
Cornelius Hackl! Who dressed up as a waiter at the Fifth Avenue Hotel the other night and took an oyster and dropped it right down Mrs . . .

Rises.

No, it's too wicked to tell you!

MRS. MOLLOY:
Oh yes, Dolly, tell it! Go on!

MRS. LEVI:
No. But it *was* Cornelius Hackl.

VANDERGELDER:
Loud.

It ain't the same man. Where'd he get the money?

MRS. LEVI:

But he's very rich.

VANDERGELDER:

Rises.

Rich! I keep his money in my own safe. He has a hundred and forty-six dollars and thirty-five cents.

MRS. LEVI:

Oh, Mr. Vandergelder, you're killing me! Do come to your senses. He's one of *the* Hackls.

MRS. MOLLOY *sits at chair right of table where Mrs. Levi has been sitting.*

VANDERGELDER:

The Hackls?

MRS. LEVI:

They built the Raritan Canal.

VANDERGELDER:

Then why should he work in my store?

MRS. LEVI:

Well, I'll tell you.

Sits at the center of the table, facing the audience.

VANDERGELDER:

Striding about.

I don't want to hear! I've got a headache! I'm going home. *It ain't the same man!!* He sleeps in my bran room. You can't get away from facts. I just made him my chief clerk.

MRS. LEVI:

If you had any sense you'd make him partner.

Rises, crosses to Mrs. Molloy.

Now Irene, I can see you were as taken with him as every-body else is.

MRS. MOLLOY:

Why, I only met him once, very hastily.

MRS. LEVI:

Yes, but I can see that you were taken with him. Now don't you be thinking of marrying him!

MRS. MOLLOY:

Her hands on her cheeks.

Dolly! What are you saying! Oh!

MRS. LEVI:

Maybe it'd be fine. But think it over carefully. He breaks hearts like hickory nuts.

VANDERGELDER:

Who?

MRS. LEVI:

Cornelius Hackl!

VANDERGELDER:

Mrs. Molloy, how often has he called on you?

MRS. MOLLOY:

Oh, I'm telling the truth. I've only seen him once in my life. Dolly Levi's been exaggerating so. I don't know where to look!

Enter MINNIE *from workroom and crosses to window.*

MINNIE:

Excuse me, Mrs. Molloy. I must get together that order for Mrs. Parkinson.

MRS. MOLLOY:

Yes, we must get that off before closing.

MINNIE:

I want to send it off by the errand girl.

Having taken a hat from the window.

Oh, I almost forgot the coat.

She starts for the wardrobe.

MRS. MOLLOY:

Running to the wardrobe to prevent her.

Oh, oh! I'll do that, Minnie!

But she is too late. MINNIE *opens the right-hand cupboard door and falls back in terror, and screams:*

MINNIE:

Oh, Mrs. Molloy! Help! There's a man!

MRS. MOLLOY *with the following speech pushes her back to the workroom door.* MINNIE *walks with one arm pointing at the cupboard. At the end of each of Mrs. Molloy's sentences she repeats—at the same pitch and degree—the words: "There's a man!"*

MRS. MOLLOY:

Slamming cupboard door.

Minnie, you imagined it. You're tired, dear. You go back in the workroom and lie down. Minnie, you're a fool; hold your tongue!

MINNIE:

There's a man!

Exit MINNIE *to workroom.*

MRS. MOLLOY *returns to the front of the stage.*

VANDERGELDER *raises his stick threateningly.*

VANDERGELDER:

If there's a man there, we'll get him out. Whoever you are, come out of there!

Strikes table with his stick.

MRS. LEVI:

Goes masterfully to the cupboard—sweeps her umbrella around among the coats and closes each door as she does so.

Nonsense! There's no man there. See! Miss Fay's nerves have been playing tricks on her. Come now, let's sit down again. What were you saying, Mr. Vandergelder?

They sit, MRS. MOLLOY *right,* MRS. LEVI *center,* VANDERGELDER *left.*

A sneeze is heard from the cupboard. They all rise, look towards cupboard, then sit again.

Well now . . .

Another tremendous sneeze.

With a gesture that says, "I can do no more":

God bless you!

They all rise. MRS. MOLLOY *stands with her back to the cupboard.*

MRS. MOLLOY:
To VANDERGELDER:

Yes, there is a man in there. I'll explain it all to you another time. Thank you very much for coming to see me. Good afternoon, Dolly. Good afternoon, Mr. Vandergelder.

VANDERGELDER:
You're protecting a man in there!

MRS. MOLLOY:
With back to cupboard.

There's a very simple explanation, but for the present, good afternoon.

BARNABY *now sneezes twice, lifting the table each time.* VANDERGELDER, *right of table, jerks off the tablecloth.* BARNABY *pulls cloth under table and rolls himself up in it.* MRS. MOLLOY *picks up the box of chocolates, which has rolled on to the floor.*

MRS. LEVI:
Lord, the whole room's *crawling* with men! I'll never get over it.

VANDERGELDER:
The world is going to pieces! I can't believe my own eyes!

MRS. LEVI:

Come, Mr. Vandergelder. Ernestina Simple is waiting for us.

VANDERGELDER:
Finds his hat and puts it on.

Mrs. Molloy, I shan't trouble you again, and *vice versa*.

MRS. MOLLOY *is standing transfixed in front of cupboard,
clasping the box of chocolates.* VANDERGELDER *snatches the
box from her and goes out.*

MRS. LEVI:
Crosses to her.

Irene, when I think of all the interesting things you have in
this room!

Kisses her.

Make the most of it, dear.

Raps cupboard.

Good-by!

Raps on table with umbrella.

Good-by!

Exit MRS. LEVI.

MRS. MOLLOY *opens door of cupboard.* CORNELIUS *steps out.*

MRS. MOLLOY:
So that was one of your practical jokes, Mr. Hackl?

CORNELIUS:
No, no, Mrs. Molloy!

MRS. MOLLOY:

Come out from under that, Barnaby Tucker, you trouble-maker!

She snatches the cloth and spreads it back on table. MINNIE *enters.*

There's nothing to be afraid of, Minnie, I know all about these gentlemen.

CORNELIUS:

Mrs. Molloy, we realize that what happened here—

MRS. MOLLOY:

You think because you're rich you can make up for all the harm you do, is that it?

CORNELIUS:

No, no!

BARNABY:

On the floor putting shoes on.

No, no!

MRS. MOLLOY:

Minnie, this is the famous Cornelius Hackl who goes round New York tying people into knots; and that's Barnaby Tucker, another troublemaker.

BARNABY:

How d'you do?

MRS. MOLLOY:

Minnie, choose yourself any hat and coat in the store. We're going out to dinner. If this Mr. Hackl is so rich and gay and charming, he's going to be rich and gay and charming to us. He dines three nights a week at the Harmonia Gardens Restaurant, does he? Well, he's taking us there now.

MINNIE:

Mrs. Molloy, are you sure it's safe?

MRS. MOLLOY:

Minnie, hold your tongue. We're in a position to put these men into jail if they so much as squeak.

CORNELIUS:

Jail, Mrs. Molloy?

MRS. MOLLOY:

Jail, Mr. Hackl. Officer Cogarty does everything I tell him to do. Minnie, you and I have been respectable for years; now we're in disgrace, we might as well make the most of it. Come into the workroom with me; I know some ways we can perk up our appearances. Gentlemen, we'll be back in a minute.

CORNELIUS:

Uh—Mrs. Molloy, I hear there's an awfully good restaurant at the railway station.

MRS. MOLLOY:

High indignation.

Railway station? Railway station? Certainly not! No, sir! You're going to give us a good dinner in the heart of the fashionable world. Go on in, Minnie! Don't you boys forget that you've made us lose our reputations, and now the fashionable world's the only place we *can* eat.

MRS. MOLLOY *exits to workroom.*

BARNABY:

She's angry at us, Cornelius. Maybe we'd better run away now.

CORNELIUS:

No, I'm going to go through with this if it kills me. Barnaby, for a woman like that a man could consent to go back to Yonkers and be a success.

BARNABY:

All I know is no woman's going to make a success out of me.

CORNELIUS:

Jail or no jail, we're going to take those ladies out to dinner. So grit your teeth.

Enter MRS. MOLLOY *and* MINNIE *from workroom dressed for the street.*

MRS. MOLLOY:

Gentlemen, the cabs are at the corner, so forward march!

She takes a hat—which will be Barnaby's at the end of Act III—and gives it to MINNIE.

CORNELIUS:

Yes, ma'am.

BARNABY *stands shaking his empty pockets warningly.*

Oh, Mrs. Molloy . . . is it far to the restaurant? Couldn't we walk?

MRS. MOLLOY:

Pauses a moment, then:

Minnie, take off your things. We're not going.

OTHERS:

Mrs. Molloy!

MRS. MOLLOY:

Mr. Hackl, I don't go anywhere I'm not wanted. Good night. I'm not very happy to have met you.

She crosses the stage as though going to the workroom door.

OTHERS:

Mrs. Molloy!

MRS. MOLLOY:

I suppose you think we're not fashionable enough for you? Well, I won't be a burden to you. Good night, Mr. Tucker.

The others follow her behind counter: CORNELIUS, BARNABY, *then* MINNIE.

CORNELIUS:

We want you to come with us more than anything in the world, Mrs. Molloy.

MRS. MOLLOY *turns and pushes the three back. They are now near the center of the stage, to the right of the table,* MRS. MOLLOY *facing the audience.*

MRS. MOLLOY:

No, you don't! Look at you! Look at the pair of them, Minnie! Scowling, both of them!

CORNELIUS:

Please, Mrs. Molloy!

MRS. MOLLOY:

Then smile.

To Barnaby.

Go on, smile! No, that's not enough. Minnie, you come with me and we'll get our own supper.

CORNELIUS:
Smile, Barnaby, you lout!

BARNABY:
My face can't smile any stronger than that.

MRS. MOLLOY:
Then do something! Show some interest. Do something lively: sing!

CORNELIUS:
I can't sing, really I can't.

MRS. MOLLOY:
We're wasting our time, Minnie. They don't want us.

CORNELIUS:
Barnaby, what can you sing? Mrs. Molloy, all we know are sad songs.

MRS. MOLLOY:
That doesn't matter. If you want us to go out with you, you've got to sing something.

All this has been very rapid; the boys turn up to counter, put their heads together, confer and abruptly turn, stand stiffly and sing "Tenting tonight; tenting tonight; tenting on the old camp ground." The four of them now repeat the refrain, softly harmonizing.

At the end of the song, after a pause, MRS. MOLLOY, *moved, says:*

MRS. MOLLOY:

We'll come!

The boys shout joyfully.

You boys go ahead.

CORNELIUS *gets his hat from counter; as he puts it on he discovers the flowers on it.* BARNABY *gets his hat from window. They go out whistling.*

MINNIE *turns and puts her hat on at the mirror.*

Minnie, get the front door key—I'll lock the workroom.

MRS. MOLLOY *goes to workroom.*

MINNIE *takes key from hook left of wardrobe and goes to Mrs. Molloy, at the workroom door. She turns her around.*

MINNIE:

Why, Mrs. Molloy, you're crying!

MRS. MOLLOY *flings her arms round Minnie.*

MRS. MOLLOY:

Oh, Minnie, the world is full of wonderful things. Watch me, dear, and tell me if my petticoat's showing.

She crosses to door, followed by MINNIE, *as—*

THE
CURTAIN
FALLS

Act III

Veranda at the Harmonia Gardens Restaurant on the Battery, New York.

This room is informal and rustic. The main restaurant is indicated to be off stage back right.

There are three entrances: swinging double doors at the center of the back wall leading to the kitchen; one on the right wall (perhaps up a few steps and flanked by potted palms) to the street; one on the left wall to the staircase leading to the rooms above.

On the stage are two tables, left and right, each with four chairs. It is now afternoon and they are not yet set for dinner.

Against the back wall is a large folding screen. Also against the back wall are hat and coat racks.

As the curtain rises, VANDERGELDER is standing, giving orders to RUDOLPH, a waiter. MALACHI STACK sits at table left.

VANDERGELDER:

Now, hear what I say. I don't want you to make any mistakes. I want a table for three.

RUDOLPH:

Tall "snob" waiter, alternating between cold superiority and rage. German accent.

For three.

VANDERGELDER:

There'll be two ladies and myself.

MALACHI:

It's a bad combination, Mr. Vandergelder. You'll regret it.

VANDERGELDER:

And I want a chicken.

MALACHI:

A chicken! You'll regret it.

VANDERGELDER:

Hold your tongue. Write it down: chicken.

RUDOLPH:

Yes, sir. Chicken Esterhazy? Chicken cacciatore? Chicken à la crème—?

VANDERGELDER:

Exploding.

A chicken! A chicken like everybody else has. And with the chicken I want a bottle of wine.

RUDOLPH:

Moselle? Chablis? Vouvray?

MALACHI:

He doesn't understand you, Mr. Vandergelder. You'd better speak louder.

VANDERGELDER:

Spelling.

W-I-N-E.

RUDOLPH:

Wine.

VANDERGELDER:

Wine! And I want this table removed. We'll eat at that table alone.

Exit RUDOLPH *through service door at back.*

MALACHI:

There are some people coming in here now, Mr. Vandergelder.

VANDERGELDER *goes to back right to look at the newcomers.*

VANDERGELDER:

What! Thunder and damnation! It's my niece Ermengarde! What's she doing here?!—Wait till I get my hands on her.

MALACHI:

Running up to him.

Mr. Vandergelder! You must keep your temper!

VANDERGELDER:

And there's that rascal artist with her. Why, it's a plot. I'll throw them in jail.

MALACHI:

Mr. Vandergelder! They're old enough to come to New York. You can't throw people into jail for coming to New York.

VANDERGELDER:

And there's Mrs. Levi! What's she doing with them? It's a plot. It's a conspiracy! What's she saying to the cabman? Go up and hear what she's saying.

MALACHI:

Listening at entrance, right.

She's telling the cabman to wait, Mr. Vandergelder. She's telling the young people to come in and have a good dinner, Mr. Vandergelder.

VANDERGELDER:

I'll put an end to this.

MALACHI:

Now, Mr. Vandergelder, if you lose your temper, you'll make matters worse. Mr. Vandergelder, come here and take my advice.

VANDERGELDER:

Stop pulling my coat. What's your advice?

MALACHI:

Hide, Mr. Vandergelder. Hide behind this screen, and listen to what they're saying.

VANDERGELDER:

Being pulled behind the screen.

Stop pulling at me.

> *They hide behind the screen as* MRS. LEVI, ERMENGARDE *and* AMBROSE *enter from the right.* AMBROSE *is carrying Ermengarde's luggage.*

ERMENGARDE:

But I don't want to eat in a restaurant. It's not proper.

MRS. LEVI:

Now, Ermengarde, dear, there's nothing wicked about eating in a restaurant. There's nothing wicked, even, about being in New York. Clergymen just make those things up to fill out their sermons.

ERMENGARDE:

Oh, I wish I were in Yonkers, where *nothing* ever happens!

MRS. LEVI:

Ermengarde, you're hungry. That's what's troubling you.

ERMENGARDE:

Anyway, after dinner you must promise to take me to Aunt Flora's. She's been waiting for me all day and she must be half dead of fright.

MRS. LEVI:

All right but of course, you know at Miss Van Huysen's you'll be back in your uncle's hands.

AMBROSE:

Hands raised to heaven.

I can't stand it.

MRS. LEVI:

To Ambrose.

Just keep telling yourself how pretty she is. Pretty girls have very little opportunity to improve their other advantages.

AMBROSE:

Listen, Ermengarde! You don't want to go back to your uncle Stop and think! That old man with one foot in the grave!

MRS. LEVI:

And the other three in the cash box.

AMBROSE:

Smelling of oats—

MRS. LEVI:

And axle grease.

MALACHI:

That's not true. It's only partly true.

VANDERGELDER:

Loudly.

Hold your tongue! I'm going to teach them a lesson.

MALACHI:

Whisper.

Keep your temper, Mr. Vandergelder. Listen to what they say.

MRS. LEVI:

Hears this; throws a quick glance toward the screen; her whole manner changes.

Oh dear, what was I saying? The Lord be praised, how glad I am that I found you two dreadful children just as you were about to break poor dear Mr. Vandergelder's heart.

AMBROSE:

He's got no heart to break!

MRS. LEVI:

Vainly signaling.

Mr. Vandergelder's a much kinder man than you think.

AMBROSE:

Kinder? He's a wolf.

MRS. LEVI:

Remember that he leads a very lonely life. Now you're going to have dinner upstairs. There are some private rooms up there,—just meant for shy timid girls like Ermengarde. Come with me.

She pushes the young people out left, AMBROSE *carrying the luggage.*

VANDERGELDER:

Coming forward.

I'll show them!

He sits at table right.

MALACHI:

Everybody should eavesdrop once in a while, I always say. There's nothing like eavesdropping to show you that the world outside your head is different from the world inside your head.

VANDERGELDER:

Producing a pencil and paper.

I want to write a note. Go and call that cabman in here. I want to talk to him.

MALACHI:

No one asks advice of a cabman, Mr. Vandergelder. They see so much of life that they have no ideas left.

VANDERGELDER:

Do as I tell you.

MALACHI:

Yes, sir. Advice of a cabman!

Exit right.

VANDERGELDER *writes his letter.*

VANDERGELDER:

"My dear Miss Van Huysen"—

To audience:

Everybody's dear in a letter. It's enough to make you give up writing 'em. "My dear Miss Van Huysen. This is Ermengarde and that rascal Ambrose Kemper. They are trying to run away. Keep them in your house until I come."

MALACHI *returns with an enormous* CABMAN *in a high hat and a long coat. He carries a whip.*

CABMAN:

Entering.

What's he want?

VANDERGELDER:

I want to talk to you.

CABMAN:

I'm engaged. I'm waiting for my parties.

VANDERGELDER:
Folding letter and writing address.

I know you are. Do you want to earn five dollars?

CABMAN:
Eh?

VANDERGELDER:
I asked you, do you want to earn five dollars?

CABMAN:
I don't know. I never tried.

VANDERGELDER:
When those parties of yours come downstairs, I want you to drive them to this address. Never mind what they say, drive them to this address. Ring the bell: give this letter to the lady of the house: see that they get in the door and keep them there.

CABMAN:
I can't make people go into a house if they don't want to.

VANDERGELDER:
Producing purse.

Can you for ten dollars?

CABMAN:
Even for ten dollars, I can't do it alone.

VANDERGELDER:
This fellow here will help you.

MALACHI:
Sitting at table left.

Now I'm pushing people into houses.

VANDERGELDER:

There's the address: Miss Flora Van Huysen, 8 Jackson Street.

CABMAN:

Even if I get them in the door I can't be sure they'll stay there.

VANDERGELDER:

For fifteen dollars you can.

MALACHI:

Murder begins at twenty-five.

VANDERGELDER:

Hold your tongue!

To cabman.

The lady of the house will help you. All you have to do is to sit in the front hall and see that the man doesn't run off with the girl. I'll be at Miss Van Huysen's in an hour or two and I'll pay you then.

CABMAN:

If they call the police, I can't do anything.

VANDERGELDER:

It's perfectly honest business. Perfectly honest.

MALACHI:

Every man's the best judge of his own honesty.

VANDERGELDER:

The young lady is my niece.

The CABMAN *laughs, skeptically.*

The young lady is my niece!!

The CABMAN *looks at Malachi and shrugs.*

She's trying to run away with a good-for-nothing and we're preventing it.

CABMAN:

Oh, I know them, sir. They'll win in the end. Rivers don't run uphill.

MALACHI:

What did I tell you, Mr. Vandergelder? Advice of a cabman.

VANDERGELDER:

Hits table with his stick.

Stack! I'll be back in half an hour. See that the table's set for three. See that nobody else eats here. Then go and join the cabman on the box.

MALACHI:

Yes, sir.

Exit VANDERGELDER *right*

CABMAN:

Who's your friend?

MALACHI:

Friend!! That's not a friend; that's an employer I'm trying out for a few days.

CABMAN:

You won't like him.

MALACHI:

I can see you're in business for yourself because you talk about liking employers. No one's ever liked an employer since business began.

CABMAN:

AW—!

MALACHI:

No, sir. I suppose you think *your horse* likes you?

CABMAN:

My old Clementine? She'd give her right feet for me.

MALACHI:

That's what all employers think. You imagine it. The streets of New York are full of cab horses winking at one another. Let's go in the kitchen and get some whiskey. I can't push people into houses when I'm sober. No, I've had about fifty employers in my life, but this is the most employer of them all. He talks to everybody as though he were paying them.

CABMAN:

I had an employer once. He watched me from eight in the morning until six at night—just sat there and watched me. Oh, dear! Even my mother didn't think I was as interesting as that.

CABMAN *exits through service door.*

MALACHI:

Following him off.

Yes, being employed is like being loved: you know that somebody's thinking about you the whole time.

Exits.

Enter right, MRS. MOLLOY, MINNIE, BARNABY *and*
CORNELIUS.

MRS. MOLLOY:

See! Here's the place I meant! Isn't it fine? Minnie, take off
your things; we'll be here for hours.

CORNELIUS:

Stopping at door.

Mrs. Molloy, are you sure you'll like it here? I think I feel a
draught.

MRS. MOLLOY:

Indeed, I do like it. We're going to have a fine dinner right in
this room; it's private, and it's elegant. Now we're all going
to forget our troubles and call each other by our first names.
Cornelius! Call the waiter.

CORNELIUS:

Wait—wait—I can't make a sound. I must have caught a cold
on that ride. Wai—No! It won't come.

MRS. MOLLOY:

I don't believe you. Barnaby, you call him.

BARNABY:

Boldly.

Waiter! Waiter!

CORNELIUS *threatens him.* BARNABY *runs left.*

MINNIE:

I never thought I'd be in such a place in my whole life. Mrs.
Molloy, is this what they call a "café"?

MRS. MOLLOY:
Sits at table left, facing audience.

Yes, this a café. Sit down, Minnie. Cornelius, Mrs. Levi gave us to understand that every waiter in New York knew you.

CORNELIUS:
They will.

BARNABY *sits at chair left;* MINNIE *in chair back to audience.*

Enter RUDOLPH *from service door.*

RUDOLPH:
Good evening, ladies and gentlemen.

CORNELIUS:
Shaking his hand.

How are you, Fritz? How are you, my friend?

RUDOLPH:
I am Rudolph.

CORNELIUS:
Of course. Rudolph, of course. Well, Rudolph, these ladies want a little something to eat—you know what I mean? Just if you can find the time—we know how busy you are.

MRS. MOLLOY:
Cornelius, there's no need to be so familiar with the waiter.

Takes menu from RUDOLPH.

CORNELIUS:
Oh, yes, there is.

MRS. MOLLOY:
Passing menu across.

Minnie, what do you want to eat?

MINNIE:
Just anything, Irene.

MRS. MOLLOY:
No, speak up, Minnie. What do you want?

MINNIE:
No, really, I have no appetite at all.

Swings round in her chair and studies the menu, horrified at the prices.

Oh . . . Oh . . . I'd like some sardines on toast and a glass of milk.

CORNELIUS:
Takes menu from her.

Great grindstones! What a sensible girl. Barnaby, shake Minnie's hand. She's the most sensible girl in the world. Rudolph, bring us gentlemen two glasses of beer, a loaf of bread and some cheese.

MRS. MOLLOY:
Takes menu.

I never heard such nonsense. Cornelius, we've come here for a good dinner and a good time. Minnie, have you ever eaten pheasant?

MINNIE:
Pheasant? No-o-o-o!

MRS. MOLLOY:
Rudolph, have you any pheasant?

RUDOLPH:

Yes, ma'am. Just in from New Jersey today.

MRS. MOLLOY:

Even the pheasants are leaving New Jersey.

She laughs loudly, pushing CORNELIUS, *then* RUDOLPH; *not from menu.*

Now, Rudolph, write this down: mock turtle soup; pheasant; mashed chestnuts; green salad; and some nice red wine.

RUDOLPH *repeats each item after her.*

CORNELIUS:

Losing all his fears, boldly.

All right, Barnaby, you watch me.

He reads from the bill of fare.

Rudolph, write this down: Neapolitan ice cream; hothouse peaches; champagne . . .

ALL:

Champagne!

BARNABY *spins round in his chair.*

CORNELIUS:

Holds up a finger.

. . . and a German band. Have you got a German band?

MRS. MOLLOY:

No, Cornelius, I won't let you be extravagant. Champagne, but no band. Now, Rudolph, be quick about this. We're hungry.

Exit RUDOLPH *to kitchen.* MRS. MOLLOY *crosses to right.*

Minnie, come upstairs. I have an idea about your hair. I think it'd be nice in two wee horns—

MINNIE:
Hurrying after her, turns and looks at the boys.

Oh! Horns!

They go out right.

There is a long pause. CORNELIUS *sits staring after them.*

BARNABY:
Cornelius, in the Army, you have to peel potatoes all the time.

CORNELIUS:
Not turning.

Oh, that doesn't matter. By the time we get out of jail we can move right over to the Old Men's Home.

Another waiter, AUGUST, *enters from service door bearing a bottle of champagne in cooler, and five glasses.* MRS. MOLLOY *re-enters right, followed by* MINNIE, *and stops* AUGUST.

MRS. MOLLOY:
Waiter! What's that? What's that you have?

AUGUST:
Young waiter; baby face; is continually bursting into tears.

It's some champagne, ma'am.

MRS. MOLLOY:

Cornelius; it's our champagne.

ALL *gather round August.*

AUGUST:

No, no. It's for His Honor the Mayor of New York and he's very impatient.

MRS. MOLLOY:

Shame on him! The Mayor of New York has more important things to be impatient about. Cornelius, open it.

CORNELIUS *takes the bottle, opens it and fills the glasses.*

AUGUST:

Ma'am, he'll kill me.

MRS. MOLLOY:

Well, have a glass first and die happy.

AUGUST:

Sits at table right, weeping.

He'll kill me.

RUDOLPH *lays the cloth on the table, left.*

MRS. MOLLOY:

I go to a public restaurant for the first time in ten years and all the waiters burst into tears. There, take that and stop crying, love.

She takes a glass to August and pats his head, then comes back.

Barnaby, make a toast!

BARNABY:

Center of the group, with naïve sincerity.

I? . . . uh . . . To all the ladies in the world . . . may I get to know more of them . . . and . . . may I get to know them better.

There is a hushed pause.

CORNELIUS:

Softly.

To the ladies!

MRS. MOLLOY:

That's *very* sweet and *very* refined. Minnie, for that I'm going to give Barnaby a kiss.

MINNIE:

Oh!

MRS. MOLLOY:

Hold your tongue, Minnie. I'm old enough to be his mother, and—

Indicating a height three feet from the floor.

a dear wee mother I would have been too. Barnaby, this is for you from all the ladies in the world.

She kisses him. BARNABY *is at first silent and dazed, then:*

BARNABY:

Now I can go back to Yonkers, Cornelius. Pudding. Pudding. Pudding!

He spins round and falls on his knees.

MRS. MOLLOY:

Look at Barnaby. He's not strong enough for a kiss. His head can't stand it.

> *Exit* AUGUST, *right service door, with tray and cooler. The sound of "Les Patineurs" waltz comes from off left.*
> CORNELIUS *sits in chair facing audience, top of table.*
> MINNIE *at left.* BARNABY *at right and* MRS. MOLLOY *back to audience.*

Minnie, I'm enjoying myself. To think that this goes on in hundreds of places every night, while I sit at home darning my stockings.

> MRS. MOLLOY *rises and dances, alone, slowly about the stage.*

Cornelius, dance with me.

CORNELIUS:

Rises.

Irene, the Hackls don't dance. We're Presbyterian.

MRS. MOLLOY:

Minnie, you dance with me.

> MINNIE *joins her.* CORNELIUS *sits again.*

MINNIE:

Lovely music.

MRS. MOLLOY:

Why, Minnie, you dance beautifully.

MINNIE:

We girls dance in the workroom when you're not looking, Irene.

MRS. MOLLOY:

You thought I'd be angry! Oh dear, no one in the world understands anyone else in the world.

The girls separate. MINNIE *dances off to her place at the table.* MRS. MOLLOY *sits thoughtfully at table right. The music fades away.*

Cornelius! Jenny Lind and all those other ladies—do you see them all the time?

CORNELIUS:

Rises and joins her at table right.

Irene, I've put them right out of my head. I'm interested in . . .

RUDOLPH *has entered by the service door. He now flings a tablecloth between them on table.*

MRS. MOLLOY:

Rudolph, what are you doing?

RUDOLPH:

A table's been reserved here. Special orders.

MRS. MOLLOY:

Stop right where you are. That party can eat inside. This veranda's ours.

RUDOLPH:

I'm very sorry. This veranda is open to anybody who wants it. Ah, there comes the man who brought the order.

Enter MALACHI *from the kitchen, drunk.*

MRS. MOLLOY:

To Malachi.

Take your table away from here. We got here first, Cornelius, throw him out.

MALACHI:

Ma'am, my employer reserved this room at four o'clock this afternoon. You can go and eat in the restaurant. My employer said it was very important that he have a table alone.

MRS. MOLLOY:

No, sir. We got here first and we're going to stay here—alone, too.

MINNIE *and* BARNABY *come forward.*

RUDOLPH:

Ladies and gentlemen!

MRS. MOLLOY:

Shut up, you!

To Malachi.

You're an impertinent, idiotic kill-joy.

MALACHI:

Very pleased.

That's an insult!

MRS. MOLLOY:

All the facts about you are insults.

To Cornelius.

Cornelius, do something. Knock it over! The table.

CORNELIUS:

Knock it over.

After a shocked struggle with himself CORNELIUS *calmly overturns the table.* AUGUST *rights the table and picks up cutlery, weeping copiously.*

RUDOLPH:

In cold fury.

I'm sorry, but this room can't be reserved for anyone. If you want to eat alone, you must go upstairs. I'm sorry, but that's the rule.

MRS. MOLLOY:

We're having a nice dinner alone and we're going to stay here. Cornelius, knock it over.

CORNELIUS *overturns the table again. The girls squeal with pleasure. The waiter* AUGUST *again scrambles for the silver.*

MALACHI:

Wait till you see my employer!

RUDOLPH:

Bringing screen down.

Ladies and gentlemen! I tell you what we'll do. There's a big screen here. We'll put the screen up between the tables. August, come and help me.

MRS. MOLLOY:

I won't eat behind a screen. I won't. Minnie, make a noise. We're not animals in a menagerie. Cornelius, no screen. Minnie, there's a fight. I feel ten years younger. No screen! No screen!

During the struggle with the screen all talk at once.

MALACHI:

Loud and clear and pointing to entrance right.

Now you'll learn something. There comes my employer now, getting out of that cab.

CORNELIUS:

Coming to him, taking off his coat.

Where? I'll knock him down too.

BARNABY *has gone up to right entrance. He turns and shouts clearly:*

BARNABY:

Cornelius, it's Wolf-trap. Yes, it is!

CORNELIUS:

Wolf-trap! Listen, everybody. I think the screen's a good idea. Have you got any more screens, Rudolph? We could use thrée or four.

He pulls the screen forward again.

MRS. MOLLOY:

Quiet down, Cornelius, and stop changing your mind. Hurry up, Rudolph, we're ready for the soup.

During the following scene RUDOLPH *serves the meal at the table left, as unobtrusively as possible.*

The stage is now divided in half. The quartet's table is at the left. Enter VANDERGELDER *from the right. Now wears overcoat and carries the box of chocolates.*

VANDERGELDER:

Stack! What's the meaning of this? I told you I wanted a table alone. What's that?

> VANDERGELDER *hits the screen twice with his stick.* MRS. MOLLOY *hits back twice with a spoon. The four young people sit:* BARNABY *facing audience;* MRS. MOLLOY *right,* MINNIE *left, and* CORNELIUS *back to audience.*

MALACHI:

Mr. Vandergelder, I did what I could. Mr. Vandergelder, you wouldn't believe what wild savages the people of New York are. There's a woman over there, Mr. Vandergelder—civilization hasn't touched her.

VANDERGELDER:

Everything's wrong. You can't even manage a thing like that. Help me off with my coat. Don't kill me. Don't kill me.

> *During the struggle with the overcoat* MR. VANDERGELDER'S *purse flies out of his pocket and falls by the screen.*
> VANDERGELDER *goes to the coat tree and hangs his coat up.*

MRS. MOLLOY:

Speak up! I can't hear you.

CORNELIUS:

My voice again. Barnaby, how's your throat? Can you speak?

BARNABY:

Can't make a sound.

MRS. MOLLOY:

Oh, all right. Bring your heads together, and we'll whisper.

VANDERGELDER:

Who are those people over there?

MALACHI:

Some city sparks and their girls, Mr. Vandergelder. What goes on in big cities, Mr. Vandergelder—best not think of it.

VANDERGELDER:

Has that couple come down from upstairs yet? I hope they haven't gone off without your seeing them.

MALACHI:

No, sir. Myself and the cabman have kept our eyes on everything.

VANDERGELDER:

Sits at right of table right, profile to the audience.

I'll sit here and wait for my guests. You go out to the cab.

MALACHI:

Yes, sir.

VANDERGELDER *unfurls newspaper and starts to read.*

MALACHI *sees the purse on the floor and picks it up.*

Eh? What's that? A purse. Did you drop something. Mr. Vandergelder?

VANDERGELDER:

No. Don't bother me any more. Do as I tell you.

MALACHI:

Stopping over. Coming center.

A purse. That fellow over there must have let it fall during the misunderstanding about the screen. No, I won't look inside. Twenty-dollar bills, dozens of them. I'll go over and give it to him.

Starts towards Cornelius, then turns and says to audience:

You're surprised? You're surprised to see me getting rid of this money so quickly, eh? I'll explain it to you. There was a time in my life when my chief interest was picking up money that didn't belong to me. The law is there to protect property, but— sure, the law doesn't care whether a property owner deserves his property or not, and the law has to be corrected. There are several thousands of people in this country engaged in correcting the law. For a while, I too was engaged in the redistribution of superfluities. A man works all his life and leaves a million to his widow. She sits in hotels and eats great meals and plays cards all afternoon and evening, with ten diamonds on her fingers. Call in the robbers! Call in the robbers! Or a man leaves it to his son who stands leaning against bars all night boring a bartender. Call in the robbers! Stealing's a weakness. There are some people who say you shouldn't have any weaknesses at all—no vices. But if a man has no vices, he's in great danger of making vices out of his virtues, and there's a spectacle. We've all seen them: men who were monsters of philanthropy and women who were dragons of purity. We've seen people who told the truth, though the Heavens fall,—and the Heavens fell. No, no—nurse one vice in your bosom. Give it the attention it deserves and let your virtues spring up modestly around it. Then you'll have the miser who's no liar; and the drunkard who's the benefactor of a whole city. Well, after I'd had that weakness of stealing for a while, I found another: I took to whisky—whisky took to me. And then I discovered an important rule that I'm going to pass on to you: Never support two weaknesses at the same time. It's your combination sinners— your lecherous liars and your miserly drunkards—who dishonor the vices and bring them into bad repute. So now you see why I want to get rid of this money: I want to keep my mind free to do the credit to whisky that it deserves. And my last word to you, ladies and gentlemen, is this: one vice at a time.

Goes over to Cornelius.

Can I speak to you for a minute?

CORNELIUS:

Rises.

You certainly can. We all want to apologize to you about that screen—that little misunderstanding.

They all rise, with exclamations of apology.

What's your name, sir?

MALACHI:

Stack, sir. Malachi Stack. If the ladies will excuse you, I'd like to speak to you for a minute.

Draws CORNELIUS *down to front of stage.*

Listen, boy, have you lost . . . ? Come here . . .

Leads him further down, out of Vandergelder's hearing.

Have you lost something?

CORNELIUS:

Mr. Stack, in this one day I've lost everything I own.

MALACHI:

There it is.

Gives him purse.

Don't mention it.

CORNELIUS:

Why, Mr. Stack . . . you know what it is? It's a miracle.

Looks toward the ceiling.

MALACHI:

Don't mention it.

CORNELIUS:

Barnaby, come here a minute. I want you to shake hands with Mr. Stack.

BARNABY, *napkin tucked into his collar, joins them.*

Mr. Stack's just found the purse I lost, Barnaby. You know— the purse full of money.

BARNABY:

Shaking his hand vigorously.

You're a wonderful man, Mr. Stack.

MALACHI:

Oh, it's nothing—nothing.

CORNELIUS:

I'm certainly glad I went to church all these years. You're a good person to know, Mr. Stack. In a way. Mr. Stack, where do you work?

MALACHI:

Well, I've just begun. I work for a Mr. Vandergelder in Yonkers.

CORNELIUS *is thunderstruck. He glances at Barnaby and turns to Malachi with awe. All three are swaying slightly, back and forth.*

CORNELIUS:

You do? It's a miracle.

He points to the ceiling.

Mr. Stack, I know you don't need it—but can I give you something for . . . for the good work?

MALACHI:
Putting out his hand.

Don't mention it. It's nothing.

Starts to go left.

CORNELIUS:

Take that.

Hands him a note.

MALACHI:
Taking note.

Don't mention it.

CORNELIUS:

And that.

Another note.

MALACHI:

Takes it and moves away.

I'd better be going.

CORNELIUS:

Oh, here. And that.

MALACHI:

Hands third note back.

No . . . I might get to like them.

Exit left.

CORNELIUS *bounds exultantly back to table.*

CORNELIUS:

Irene, I feel a lot better about everything. Irene, I feel so well that I'm going to tell the truth.

MRS. MOLLOY:

I'd forgotten that, Minnie. Men get drunk so differently from women. All right, what is the truth?

CORNELIUS:

If I tell the truth, will you let me . . . will you let me put my arm around your waist?

MINNIE *screams and flings her napkin over her face.*

MRS. MOLLOY:

Hold your tongue, Minnie. All right, you can put your arm around my waist just to show it can be done in a gentlemanly way; but I might as well warn you: a corset is a corset.

CORNELIUS:

His arm around her; softly.

You're a wonderful person, Mrs. Molloy.

MRS. MOLLOY:
Thank you.

She removes his hand from around her waist.

All right, now that's enough. What is the truth?

CORNELIUS:
Irene, I'm not rich as Mrs. Levi said I was.

MRS. MOLLOY:
Not rich!

CORNELIUS:
I almost never came to New York. And I'm not like she said I was,—bad. And I think you ought to know that at this very minute Mr. Vandergelder's sitting on the other side of that screen.

MRS. MOLLOY:
What!! Well, he's not going to spoil any party of mine. So *that's* why we've been whispering? Let's forget all about Mr. Vandergelder and have some more wine.

They start to sing softly: "The Sidewalks of New York."

Enter MRS. LEVI, *from the street, in an elaborate dress.*
VANDERGELDER *rises.*

MRS. LEVI:
Good evening, Mr. Vandergelder.

VANDERGELDER:

Where's—where's Miss Simple?

MRS. LEVI:

Mr. Vandergelder, I'll never trust a woman again as long as I live.

VANDERGELDER:

Well? What is it?

MRS. LEVI:

She ran away this afternoon and got married!

VANDERGELDER:

She did?

MRS. LEVI:

Married, Mr. Vandergelder, to a young boy of fifty.

VANDERGELDER:

She did?

MRS. LEVI:

Oh, I'm as disappointed as you are. I-can't-eat-a-thing-what-have-you-ordered?

VANDERGELDER:

I ordered what you told me to, a chicken.

Enter AUGUST. *He goes to Vandergelder's table.*

MRS. LEVI:

I don't think I could face a chicken. Oh, waiter. How do you do? What's your name?

AUGUST:

August, ma'am.

MRS. LEVI:

August, this is Mr. Vandergelder of Yonkers—Yonkers' most influential citizen, in fact. I want you to see that he's served with the best you have and served promptly. And there'll only be the two of us.

MRS. LEVI gives one set of cutlery to AUGUST.
VANDERGELDER puts chocolate box under table.

Mr. Vandergelder's been through some trying experiences today—what with men hidden all over Mrs. Molloy's store—like Indians in ambush.

VANDERGELDER:

Between his teeth.

Mrs. Levi, you don't have to tell him everything about me.

The quartet commences singing again very softly.

MRS. LEVI:

Mr. Vandergelder, if you're thinking about getting married, you might as well learn right now you have to let women be women. Now, August, we want excellent service.

AUGUST:

Yes, ma'am.

Exits to kitchen.

VANDERGELDER:

You've managed things very badly. When I plan a thing it takes place.

MRS. LEVI rises.

Where are you going?

MRS. LEVI:

Oh, I'd just like to see who's on the other side of that screen.

MRS. LEVI *crosses to the other side of the stage and sees the quartet. They are frightened and fall silent.*

CORNELIUS:

Rising.

Good evening, Mrs. Levi.

MRS. LEVI *takes no notice, but, taking up the refrain where they left off, returns to her place at the table right.*

VANDERGELDER:

Well, who was it?

MRS. LEVI:

Oh, just some city sparks entertaining their girls, I guess.

VANDERGELDER:

Always wanting to know everything; always curious about everything; always putting your nose into other people's affairs. Anybody who lived with you would get as nervous as a cat.

MRS. LEVI:

What? What's that you're saying?

VANDERGELDER:

I said anybody who lived with you would—

MRS. LEVI:

Horace Vandergelder, get that idea right out of your head this minute. I'm surprised that you even mentioned such a thing. Understand once and for all that I have no intention of marrying you.

VANDERGELDER:

I didn't mean that.

MRS. LEVI:

You've been hinting around at such a thing for some time, but from now on put such ideas right out of your head.

VANDERGELDER:

Stop talking that way. That's not what I meant at all.

MRS. LEVI:

I hope not. I should hope not. Horace Vandergelder, you go your way

Points a finger.

and I'll go mine.

Points again in same direction.

I'm not some Irene Molloy, whose head can be turned by a pot of geraniums. Why, the idea of your even suggesting such a thing.

VANDERGELDER:

Mrs. Levi, you misunderstood me.

MRS. LEVI:

I certainly hope I did. If I had any intention of marrying again it would be to a far more pleasure-loving man than you. Why I'd marry Cornelius Hackl before I'd marry you.

CORNELIUS *raises his head in alarm. The others stop eating and listen.*

However, we won't discuss it any more.

Enter AUGUST *with a tray.*

Here's August with our food. I'll serve it, August.

AUGUST:
Yes, ma'am.

Exit AUGUST.

MRS. LEVI:
Here's some white meat for you, and some giblets, very tender and very good for you. No, as I said before, you go your way and I'll go mine.—Start right in on the wine. I think you'll feel better at once. However, since you brought the matter up, there's one more thing I think I ought to say.

VANDERGELDER:
Rising in rage.

I didn't bring the matter up at all.

MRS. LEVI:
We'll have forgotten all about it in a moment, but—sit down, sit down, we'll close the matter forever in just a moment, but there's one more thing I ought to say:

VANDERGELDER *sits down.*

It's true, I'm a woman who likes to know everything that's going on; who likes to manage things, you're perfectly right about that. But I wouldn't like to manage anything as disorderly as your household, as out of control, as untidy. You'll have to do that yourself, God helping you.

VANDERGELDER:
It's not out of control.

MRS. LEVI:

Very well, let's not say another word about it. Take some more of that squash, it's good. No, Horace, a complaining, quarrelsome, friendless soul like you is no sort of companion for me. You go your way

Peppers her own plate.

and I'll go mine.

Peppers his plate.

VANDERGELDER:

Stop saying that.

MRS. LEVI:

I won't say another word.

VANDERGELDER:

Besides . . . I'm not those things you said I am.

MRS. LEVI:

What?—Well, I guess you're friendless, aren't you? Ermengarde told me this morning you'd even quarreled with your barber—a man who's held a razor to your throat for twenty years! Seems to me that that's sinking pretty low.

VANDERGELDER:

Well, . . . but . . . my clerks, they . . .

MRS. LEVI:

They like you? Cornelius Hackl and that Barnaby? Behind your back they call you Wolf-trap.

Quietly the quartet at the other table have moved up to the screens—bringing chairs for Mrs. Molloy and Minnie. Wine glasses in hand, they overhear this conversation.

VANDERGELDER:

Blanching.

They don't.

MRS. LEVI:

No, Horace. It looks to me as though I were the last person in the world that liked you, and even I'm just so-so. No, for the rest of my life I intend to have a good time. You'll be able to find some housekeeper who can prepare you three meals for a dollar a day—it can be done, you know, if you like cold baked beans. You'll spend your last days listening at keyholes, for fear someone's cheating you. Take some more of that.

VANDERGELDER:

Dolly, you're a damned exasperating woman.

MRS. LEVI:

There! You see? That's the difference between us. I'd be nagging you all day to get some spirit into you. You could be a perfectly charming, witty, amiable man, if you wanted to.

VANDERGELDER:

Rising, bellowing.

I don't want to be charming.

MRS. LEVI:

But you are. Look at you now. You can't hide it.

VANDERGELDER:

Sits.

Listening at keyholes! Dolly, you have no right to say such things to me.

MRS. LEVI:

At your age you ought to enjoy hearing the honest truth.

VANDERGELDER:

My age! My age! You're always talking about my age.

MRS. LEVI:

I don't know what your age is, but I do know that up at Yonkers with bad food and bad temper you'll double it in six months. Let's talk of something else; but before we leave the subject there's one more thing I *am* going to say.

VANDERGELDER:

Don't!

MRS. LEVI:

Sometimes, just sometimes, I think I'd be tempted to marry you out of sheer pity; and if the confusion in your house gets any worse I may *have* to.

VANDERGELDER:

I haven't asked you to marry me.

MRS. LEVI:

Well, *please don't.*

VANDERGELDER:

And my house is not in confusion.

MRS. LEVI:

What? With your niece upstairs in the restaurant right now?

VANDERGELDER:

I've fixed that better than you know.

MRS. LEVI:

And your clerks skipping around New York behind your back?

VANDERGELDER:

They're in Yonkers where they always are.

MRS. LEVI:

Nonsense!

VANDERGELDER:

What do you mean, nonsense?

MRS. LEVI:

Cornelius Hackl's the other side of that screen this very minute.

VANDERGELDER:

It ain't the same man!

MRS. LEVI:

All right. Go on. Push it, knock it down. Go and see.

VANDERGELDER:

Goes to screen, pauses in doubt, then returns to his chair again.

I don't believe it.

MRS. LEVI:

All right. All right. Eat your chicken. Of course, Horace, if your affairs went from bad to worse and you became actually miserable, I might feel that it was my duty to come up to Yonkers and be of some assistance to you. After all, I was your wife's oldest friend.

VANDERGELDER:

I don't know how you ever got any such notion. Now understand, once and for all, I have *no intention of marrying anybody.* Now, I'm tired and I don't want to talk.

CORNELIUS *crosses to extreme left,* MRS. MOLLOY *following him.*

MRS. LEVI:

I won't say another word, either.

CORNELIUS:

Irene, I think we'd better go. You take this money and pay the bill. Oh, don't worry, it's not mine.

MRS. MOLLOY:

No, no, I'll tell you what we'll do. You boys put on our coats and veils, and if he comes stamping over here, he'll think you're girls.

CORNELIUS:

What! Those things!

MRS. MOLLOY:

Yes. Come on.

She and MINNIE *take the clothes from the stand.*

VANDERGELDER:
Rises.

I've got a headache. I've had a bad day. I'm going to Flora Van Huysen's, and then I'm going back to my hotel.

Reaches for his purse.

So, here's the money to pay for the dinner.

Searching another pocket.

Here's the money to pay for the . . .

Going through all his pockets.

Here's the money . . . I've lost my purse!!

MRS. LEVI:

Impossible! I can't imagine you without your purse.

VANDERGELDER:

It's been stolen.

Searching overcoat.

Or I left it in the cab. What am I going to do? I'm new at the hotel; they don't know me. I've never been here before. . . . Stop eating the chicken, I can't pay for it!

MRS. LEVI:

Laughing gaily.

Horace, I'll be able to find some money. Sit down and calm yourself.

VANDERGELDER:

Dolly Gallagher, I gave you twenty-five dollars this morning.

MRS. LEVI:

I haven't a cent. I gave it to my lawyer. We can borrow it from Ambrose Kemper, upstairs.

VANDERGELDER:

I wouldn't take it.

MRS. LEVI:

Cornelius Hackl will lend it to us.

VANDERGELDER:

He's in Yonkers.—Waiter!

CORNELIUS *comes forward dressed in Mrs. Molloy's coat, thrown over his shoulder like a cape.*

MRS. LEVI *is enjoying herself immensely.* VANDERGELDER *again goes to back wall to examine the pockets of his overcoat.*

MRS. MOLLOY:

Cornelius, is that Mr. Vandergelder's purse?

CORNELIUS:

I didn't know it myself. I thought it was money just wandering around loose that didn't belong to anybody.

MRS. MOLLOY:

Goodness! That's what politicians think!

VANDERGELDER:

Waiter!

A band off left starts playing a polka. BARNABY *comes forward dressed in Minnie's hat, coat and veil.*

MINNIE:

Irene, doesn't Barnaby make a lovely girl? He just ought to stay that way.

MRS. LEVI *and* VANDERGELDER *move their table upstage while searching for the purse.*

MRS. MOLLOY:

Why should we have our evening spoiled? Cornelius, I can teach you to dance in a few minutes. Oh, he won't recognize you.

MINNIE:

Barnaby, it's the easiest thing in the world.

They move their table up against the back wall.

MRS. LEVI:

Horace, you danced with me at your wedding and you danced with me at mine. Do you remember?

VANDERGELDER:

No. Yes.

MRS. LEVI:

Horace, you were a good dancer then. Don't confess to me that you're too old to dance.

VANDERGELDER:

Not too old. I just don't want to dance.

MRS. LEVI:

Listen to that music. Horace, do you remember the dances in the firehouse at Yonkers on Saturday nights? You gave me a fan. Come, come on!

VANDERGELDER *and* MRS. LEVI *start to dance.* CORNELIUS, *dancing with* MRS. MOLLOY, *bumps into Vandergelder, back to back.* VANDERGELDER, *turning, fails at first to recognize him, then does and roars:*

VANDERGELDER:

You're discharged! Not a word! You're fired! Where's that idiot, Barnaby Tucker? He's fired, too.

The four young people, laughing, start rushing out the door to the street. VANDERGELDER, *pointing at Mrs. Molloy, shouts:*

You're discharged!

MOLLOY:

Pointing at him.

You're discharged!

Exit.

VANDERGELDER:

You're discharged!

Enter from left, AMBROSE *and* ERMENGARDE.
To Ermengarde.

I'll lock you up for the rest of your life, young lady.

ERMENGARDE:

Uncle!

She faints in AMBROSE'S *arms.*

VANDERGELDER:

To Ambrose.

I'll have you arrested. Get out of my sight. I never want to see you again.

AMBROSE:

Carrying ERMENGARDE *across to exit right.*

You can't do anything to me, Mr. Vandergelder.

Exit AMBROSE *and* ERMENGARDE.

MRS. LEVI:

Who has been laughing heartily, follows the distraught VANDERGELDER *about the stage as he continues to hunt for his purse.*

Well, there's your life, Mr. Vandergelder! Without niece—without clerks—without bride—and without your purse. *Will you marry me now?*

VANDERGELDER:

No!

To get away from her, he dashes into the kitchen.
MRS. LEVI, *still laughing, exclaims to the audience:*

MRS. LEVI:

Damn!!

And rushes off right.

THE
CURTAIN
FALLS

Act IV

Miss Flora Van Huysen's house.

This is a prosperous spinster's living room and is filled with knickknacks, all in bright colors, and hung with family portraits, bird cages, shawls, etc.

There is only one entrance—a large double door in the center of the back wall. Beyond it one sees the hall which leads left to the street door and right to the kitchen and the rest of the house. On the left are big windows hung with lace curtains on heavy draperies. Front left is Miss Van Huysen's sofa, covered with bright-colored cushions, and behind it a table. On the right is another smaller sofa. MISS VAN HUYSEN *is lying on the sofa. The* COOK *is at the window, left.* MISS VAN HUYSEN, *fifty, florid, stout and sentimental, is sniffing at smelling salts.* COOK *(enormous) holds a china mixing bowl.*

COOK:

No, ma'am. I could swear I heard a cab drawing up to the door.

MISS VAN H.:

You imagined it. Imagination. Everything in life . . . like that . . . disappointment . . . illusion. Our plans . . . our hopes . . . what becomes of them? Nothing. The story of my life.

She sings for a moment.

COOK:

Pray God nothing's happened to the dear girl. Is it a long journey from Yonkers?

MISS VAN H.:

No; but long enough for a thousand things to happen.

COOK:

Well, we've been waiting all day. Don't you think we ought to call the police about it?

MISS VAN H.:

The police! If it's God's will, the police can't prevent it. Oh, in three days, in a week, in a year, we'll know what's happened. . . . And if anything *has* happened to Ermengarde, it'll be a lesson to *him*—that's what it'll be.

COOK:

To who?

MISS VAN H.:

To that cruel uncle of hers, of course,—to Horace Vandergelder, and to everyone else who tries to separate young lovers. Young lovers have enough to contend with as it is. Who should know that better than I? No one. The story of my life.

Sings for a moment, then:

There! Now I hear a cab. Quick!

COOK:

No. No, ma'am. I don't see anything.

MISS VAN H.:

There! What did I tell you? Everything's imagination—illusion.

COOK:

But surely, if they'd çhanged their plans Mr. Vandergelder would have sent you a message.

MISS VAN H.:

Oh, I know what's the matter. That poor child probably thought she was coming to another prison—to another tyrant. If she'd known that I was her friend, and a friend of all young lovers, she'd be here by now. Oh, yes, she would. Her life shall not be crossed with obstacles and disappointments as . . . Cook, a minute ago my smelling salts were on this table. Now they've completely disappeared.

COOK:

Why, there they are, ma'am, right there in your hand.

MISS VAN H.:

Goodness! How did they get there? I won't inquire. Stranger things have happened!

COOK:

I suppose Mr. Vandergelder was sending her down with someone?

MISS VAN H.:

Two can go astray as easily as . . .

She sneezes.

COOK:

God bless you!

Runs to window.

Now, here's a carriage stopping.

The doorbell rings.

MISS VAN H.:

Well, open the door, Cook.

COOK *exits.*

It's probably some mistake . . .

Sneezes again.

God bless you!

Sounds of altercation off in hall.

It almost sounds as though I heard voices.

CORNELIUS:

Off.

I don't want to come in. This is a free country, I tell you.

CABMAN:

Off.

Forward march!

MALACHI:

Off.

In you go. We have orders.

CORNELIUS:

Off.

You can't make a person go where he doesn't want to go.

Enter MALACHI, *followed by* COOK. *The* CABMAN *bundles* BARNABY *and* CORNELIUS *into the room, but they fight their way back into the hall.* CORNELIUS *has lost Mrs. Molloy's coat, but* BARNABY *is wearing Minnie's clothes.*

MALACHI:

Begging your pardon, ma'am, are you Miss Van Huysen?

MISS VAN H.:

Yes, I am, unfortunately. What's all this noise about?

MALACHI:

There are two people here that Mr. Vandergelder said must be brought to this house and kept here until he comes. And here's his letter to you.

MISS VAN H.:

No one has any right to tell me whom I'm to keep in my house if they don't want to stay.

MALACHI:

You're right, ma'am. Everybody's always talking about people breaking into houses, ma'am; but there are more people in the world who want to break out of houses, that's what I always say.—Bring them in, Joe.

Enter CORNELIUS *and* BARNABY *being pushed by the* CABMAN.

CORNELIUS:

This young lady and I have no business here. We jumped into a cab and asked to be driven to the station and these men brought us to the house and forced us to come inside. There's been a mistake.

CABMAN:

Is your name Miss Van Huysen?

MISS VAN H.:

Everybody's asking me if my name's Miss Van Huysen. I think that's a matter I can decide for myself. Now will you all be quiet while I read this letter?. . . "This is Ermengarde and that rascal Ambrose Kemper . . . " Now I know who you two are, anyway. "They are trying to run away . . . " Story of my life. "Keep them in your house until I come." Mr. Kemper, you have nothing to fear.

To Cabman.

Who are you?

CABMAN:

I'm Joe. I stay here until the old man comes. He owes me fifteen dollars.

MALACHI:

That's right, Miss Van Huysen, we must stay here to see they don't escape.

MISS VAN H.:
To Barnaby

My dear child, take off your things. We'll all have some coffee.

To Malachi and cabman.

You two go out and wait in the hall. I'll send coffee out to you. Cook, take them.

COOK *pushes* MALACHI *and* CABMAN *into the hall.*

CORNELIUS:

Ma'am, we're not the people you're expecting, and there's no reason . . .

MISS VAN H.:

Mr. Kemper, I'm not the tyrant you think I am. . . . You don't have to be afraid of me. . . . I know you're trying to run away with this innocent girl. . . . All my life I have suffered from the interference of others. You shall not suffer as I did. So put yourself entirely in my hands.

She lifts Barnaby's veil.

Ermengarde!

Kisses him on both cheeks.

Where's your luggage?

BARNABY:

It's—uh—uh—it's . . .

CORNELIUS:

Oh, I'll find it in the morning. It's been mislaid.

MISS VAN H.:

Mislaid! How like life! Well, Ermengarde; you shall put on some of my clothes.

BARNABY:

Oh, I know I wouldn't be happy, really.

MISS VAN H.:

She's a shy little thing, isn't she? Timid little darling! . . . Cook! Put some gingerbread in the oven and get the coffee ready . . .

COOK:

Yes, ma'am.

Exits to kitchen.

MISS VAN H.:

. . . while I go and draw a good hot bath for Ermengarde.

CORNELIUS:

Oh, oh—Miss Van Huysen . . .

MISS VAN H.:

Believe me, Ermengarde, your troubles are at an end. You two will be married tomorrow.

To Barnaby.

My dear, you look just like I did at your age, and your sufferings have been as mine. While you're bathing, I'll come and tell you the story of my life.

BARNABY:

Oh, I don't want to take a bath. I always catch cold.

MISS VAN H.:

No, dear, you won't catch cold. I'll slap you all over. I'll be back in a minute.

Exit.

CORNELIUS:

Looking out of window.

Barnaby, do you think we could jump down from this window?

BARNABY:

Yes—we'd kill ourselves.

CORNELIUS:

We'll just have to stay here and watch for something to happen. Barnaby, the situation's desperate.

BARNABY:

It began getting desperate about half-past four and it's been getting worse ever since. Now I have to take a bath and get slapped all over.

Enter MISS VAN HUYSEN *from kitchen.*

MISS VAN H.:

Ermengarde, you've still got those wet things on. Your bath's nearly ready. Mr. Kemper, you come into the kitchen and put your feet in the oven.

The doorbell rings. Enter COOK.

What's that? It's the doorbell. I expect it's your uncle.

COOK:

There's the doorbell.

At window.

It's *another* man and a girl in a cab!

MISS VAN H.:

Well, go and let them in, Cook. Now, come with me, you two. Come, Ermengarde.

Exit COOK. MISS VAN HUYSEN *drags* CORNELIUS *and the protesting* BARNABY *off into the kitchen.*

COOK:

Off.

No, that's impossible. Come in, anyway.

Enter ERMENGARDE, *followed by* AMBROSE, *carrying the two pieces of luggage.*

There's some mistake. I'll tell Miss Van Huysen, but there's some mistake.

ERMENGARDE:

But, I tell you, I *am* Mr. Vandergelder's niece; I'm Ermengarde.

COOK:

Beg your pardon, Miss, but you *can't* be Miss Ermengarde.

ERMENGARDE:

But—but—here I *am*. And that's my baggage.

COOK:

Well, I'll tell Miss Van Huysen who you *think* you are, but she won't like it.

Exits.

AMBROSE:

You'll be all right now, Ermengarde. I'd better go before she sees me.

ERMENGARDE:

Oh, no. You must stay. I feel so strange here.

AMBROSE:

I know, but Mr. Vandergelder will be here in a minute. . . .

ERMENGARDE:

Ambrose, you can't go. You can't leave me in this crazy house with those drunken men in the hall. Ambrose . . . Ambrose, let's say you're someone else that my uncle sent down to take care of me. Let's say you're—you're Cornelius Hackl!

AMBROSE:

Who's Cornelius Hackl?

ERMENGARDE:

You know. He's chief clerk in Uncle's store.

AMBROSE:

I don't want to be Cornelius Hackl. No, no, Ermengarde, come away with me now. I'll take you to my friend's house. Or I'll take you to Mrs. Levi's house.

ERMENGARDE:

Why, it was Mrs. Levi who threw us right at Uncle Horace's face. Oh, I wish I were back in Yonkers where nothing ever happens.

Enter MISS VAN HUYSEN.

MISS VAN H.:

What's all this I hear? Who do you say you are?

ERMENGARDE:

Aunt Flora . . . don't you remember me? I'm Ermengarde.

MISS VAN H.:

And you're Mr. Vandergelder's niece?

ERMENGARDE:

Yes, I am.

MISS VAN H.:

Well, that's very strange indeed, because he has just sent me another niece named Ermengarde. She came with a letter from him, explaining everything. Have you got a letter from him?

ERMENGARDE:

No . . .

MISS VAN H.:

Really!—And who is this?

ERMENGARDE:

This is Cornelius Hackl, Aunt Flora.

MISS VAN H.:

Never heard of him.

ERMENGARDE:

He's chief clerk in Uncle's store.

MISS VAN H.:

Never heard of him. The other Ermengarde came with the man she's in love with, and that *proves* it. She came with Mr. Ambrose Kemper.

AMBROSE:

Shouts.

Ambrose Kemper!

MISS VAN H.:

Yes, Mr. Hackl, and Mr. Ambrose Kemper is in the kitchen there now *with his feet in the oven.*

ERMENGARDE *starts to cry.* MISS VAN HUYSEN *takes her to the sofa. They both sit.*

Dear child, what is your trouble?

ERMENGARDE:

Oh, dear. I don't know what to do.

MISS VAN H.:

In a low voice.

Are you in love with this man?

ERMENGARDE:

Yes, I am.

MISS VAN H.:

I could see it—and are people trying to separate you?

ERMENGARDE:

Yes, they are.

MISS VAN H.:

I could see it—who? Horace Vandergelder?

ERMENGARDE:

Yes.

MISS VAN H.:

That's enough for me. I'll put a stop to Horace Vandergelder's goings on.

MISS VAN HUYSEN *draws* AMBROSE *down to sit on her other side.*

Mr. Hackl, think of me as your friend. Come in the kitchen and get warm. . . .

She rises and starts to go out.

We can decide later who everybody is. My dear, would you like a good hot bath?

ERMENGARDE:

Yes, I would.

MISS VAN H.:

Well, when Ermengarde comes out you can go in.

Enter CORNELIUS *from the kitchen.*

CORNELIUS:

Oh, Miss Van Huysen . . .

ERMENGARDE:

Why, Mr. Hack—!!

CORNELIUS:

Sliding up to her, urgently.

Not yet! I'll explain. I'll explain everything.

MISS VAN H.:

Mr. Kemper!—Mr. Kemper! This is Mr. Cornelius Hackl.

To Ambrose.

Mr. Hackl, this is Mr. Ambrose Kemper.

Pause, while the men glare at one another.

Perhaps you two know one another?

AMBROSE:

No!

CORNELIUS:
No, we don't.

AMBROSE:

Hotly.

Miss Van Huysen, I know that man is not Ambrose Kemper.

CORNELIUS:
Ditto.

And he's not Cornelius Hackl.

MISS VAN H.:
My dear young men, what does it matter what your names are? The important thing is that you are you.

To Ambrose.

You are alive and breathing, aren't you, Mr. Hackl?

Pinches Ambrose's left arm.

AMBROSE:
Ouch, Miss Van Huysen.

MISS VAN H.:
This dear child imagines she is Horace Vandergelder's niece Ermengarde.

ERMENGARDE:
But I am.

MISS VAN H.:
The important thing is that you're all in love. Everything else is illusion.

She pinches Cornelius' arm.

CORNELIUS:

Ouch! Miss Van Huysen!

MISS VAN H.:

Comes down and addresses the audience.

Everybody keeps asking me if I'm Miss Van Huys . . .

She seems suddenly to be stricken with doubt as to who she is; her face shows bewildered alarm. She pinches herself on the upper arm and is abruptly and happily relieved.

Now, you two gentlemen sit down and have a nice chat while this dear child has a good hot bath.

The doorbell rings ERMENGARDE *exit,* MISS VAN HUYSEN *about to follow her, but stops. Enter* COOK.

COOK:

There's the doorbell again.

MISS VAN H.:

Well, answer it.

She and ERMENGARDE *exit to kitchen.*

COOK:

At window, very happy about all these guests.

It's a cab and three ladies. I never saw such a night.

Exit to front door.

MISS VAN H.:

Gentlemen, you can rest easy. I'll see that Mr. Vandergelder lets his nieces marry you both.

Enter MRS. LEVI.

MRS. LEVI:

Flora, how are you?

MISS VAN H.:

Dolly Gallagher! What brings you here?

MRS. LEVI:

Great Heavens, Flora, what are those two drunken men doing in your hall?

MISS VAN H.:

I don't know. Horace Vandergelder sent them to me.

MRS. LEVI:

Well, I've brought you two girls in much the same condition. Otherwise they're the finest girls in the world.

She goes up to the door and leads in MRS. MOLLOY. MINNIE *follows.*

I want you to meet Irene Molloy and Minnie Fay.

MISS VAN H.:

Delighted to know you.

MRS. LEVI:

Oh, I see you two gentlemen are here, too. Mr. Hackl, I was about to look for you

Pointing about the room.

somewhere here.

CORNELIUS:

No, Mrs. Levi. I'm ready to face anything now.

MRS. LEVI:

Mr. Vandergelder will be here in a minute. He's downstairs trying to pay for a cab without any money.

MRS. MOLLOY:

Holding Vandergelder's purse.

Oh, I'll help him.

MRS. LEVI:

Yes, will you, dear? You had to pay the restaurant bills. You must have hundreds of dollars there it seems.

MRS. MOLLOY:

This is his own purse he lost. I can't give it back to him without seeming . . . .

MRS. LEVI:

I'll give it back to him.—There, you help him with this now.

She gives Mrs. Molloy a bill and puts the purse airily under her arm.

VANDERGELDER:

Off.

Will somebody please pay for this cab?

MRS. MOLLOY *exits to front door.*

MRS. MOLLOY:

Off stage.

I'll take care of that, Mr. Vandergelder.

As MR. VANDERGELDER *enters,* MALACHI *and the* CABMAN *follow him in.* VANDERGELDER *carries overcoat, stick and box of chocolates.*

CABMAN:

Fifteen dollars, Mr. Vandergelder.

MALACHI:

Hello, Mr. Vandergelder.

VANDERGELDER:

To Malachi.

You're discharged!

To Cabman.

You too!

MALACHI *and* CABMAN *go out and wait in the ball.*

So I've caught up with you at last!

To Ambrose.

I never want to see you again!

To Cornelius.

You're discharged! Get out of the house, both of you.

He strikes sofa with his stick; a second after, MISS VAN HUYSEN *strikes him on the shoulder with a folded newspaper or magazine.*

MISS VAN H.:

Forcefully.

Now then you. Stop ordering people out of my house. You can shout and carry on in Yonkers, but when you're in my house you'll behave yourself.

VANDERGELDER:

They're both dishonest scoundrels.

MISS VAN H.:

Take your hat off. Gentlemen, you stay right where you are.

CORNELIUS:

Mr. Vandergelder, I can explain—

MISS VAN H.:

There aren't going to be any explanations. Horace, stop scowling at Mr. Kemper and forgive him.

VANDERGELDER:

That's not Kemper, that's a dishonest rogue named Cornelius Hackl.

MISS VAN H.:

You're crazy.

Points to Ambrose.

That's Cornelius Hackl.

VANDERGELDER:

I guess I know my own chief clerk.

MISS VAN H.:

I don't care what their names are. You shake hands with them both, or out you go.

VANDERGELDER:

Shake hands with those dogs and scoundrels!

MRS. LEVI:

Mr. Vandergelder, you've had a hard day. You don't want to go out in the rain now. Just for form's sake, you shake hands with them. You can start quarreling with them tomorrow.

VANDERGELDER:

Gives CORNELIUS *one finger to shake.*

There! Don't regard that as a handshake.

He turns to AMBROSE, *who mockingly offers him one finger.*

Hey! I never want to see you again.

MRS. MOLLOY *enters from front door.*

MRS. MOLLOY:

Miss Van Huysen.

MISS VAN H.:

Yes, dear?

MRS. MOLLOY:

Do I smell coffee?

MISS VAN H.:

Yes, dear.

MRS. MOLLOY:

Can I have some, good and black?

MISS VAN H.:

Come along, everybody. We'll all go into the kitchen and have some coffee.

As they all go:

Horace, you'll be interested to know there are two Ermengardes in there. . . .

VANDERGELDER:

Two!!

Last to go is MINNIE, *who revolves about the room dreamily waltzing, a finger on her forehead.* MRS. LEVI *has been standing at one side. She now comes forward, in thoughtful mood.* MINNIE *continues her waltz round the left sofa and out to the kitchen.*

MRS. LEVI, *left alone, comes to front, addressing an imaginary Ephraim.*

MRS. LEVI:

Ephraim Levi, I'm going to get married again. Ephraim, I'm marrying Horace Vandergelder for his money. I'm going to send his money out doing all the things you taught me. Oh, it won't be a marriage in the sense that we had one—but I shall certainly make him happy, and Ephraim—I'm tired. I'm tired of living from hand to mouth, and I'm asking your permission, Ephraim—will you give me away?

Now addressing the audience, she holds up the purse.

Money! Money!—it's like the sun we walk under; it can kill or cure.—Mr. Vandergelder's money! Vandergelder's never tired of saying most of the people in the world are fools, and in a way he's right, isn't he? Himself, Irene, Cornelius, myself! But there comes a moment in everybody's life when he must decide whether he'll live among human beings or not—a fool among fools or a fool alone.

As for me, I've decided to live among them.

I wasn't always so. After my husband's death I retired into myself. Yes, in the evenings, I'd put out the cat, and I'd lock the door, and I'd make myself a little rum toddy; and before I went to bed I'd say a little prayer, thanking God that I was independent—that no one else's life was mixed up with mine. And when ten o'clock sounded from Trinity Church tower, I fell off to sleep and I was a perfectly contented woman. And one night, after two years of this, an oak leaf fell out of my Bible. I had placed it there on the day my husband asked me to marry him; a perfectly good oak leaf—but without color and without life. And suddenly I realized that for a long time I had not shed one tear; nor had I been filled with the wonderful hope that something or other would turn out well. I saw that I was like that oak leaf, and on that night I decided to rejoin the human race.

Yes, we're all fools and we're all in danger of destroying the world with our folly. But the surest way to keep us out of harm is to give us the four or five human pleasures that are our right in the world,—and that takes a little *money!*

The difference between a little money and no money at all is enormous—and can shatter the world. And the difference between a little money and an enormous amount of money is very slight—and that, also, can shatter the world.

Money, I've always felt, money—pardon my expression—is like manure; it's not worth a thing unless it's spread about encouraging young things to grow.

Anyway,—that's the opinion of the second Mrs. Vandergelder.

VANDERGELDER *enters with two cups of coffee. With his back, he closes both doors.*

VANDERGELDER:
Miss Van Huysen asked me to bring you this.

MRS. LEVI:
Thank you both. Sit down and rest yourself. What's been going on in the kitchen?

VANDERGELDER:

A lot of foolishness. Everybody falling in love with everybody. I forgave 'em; Ermengarde and that artist.

MRS. LEVI:

I knew you would.

VANDERGELDER:

I made Cornelius Hackl my partner.

MRS. LEVI:

You won't regret it.

VANDERGELDER:

Dolly, you said some mighty unpleasant things to me in the restaurant tonight . . . all that about my house . . . and everything.

MRS. LEVI:

Let's not say another word about it.

VANDERGELDER:

Dolly, you have a lot of faults—

MRS. LEVI:

Oh, I know what you mean.

VANDERGELDER:

You're bossy, scheming, inquisitive . . .

MRS. LEVI:

Go on.

VANDERGELDER:

But you're a wonderful woman. Dolly, marry me.

MRS. LEVI:

Horace!

Rises.

Stop right there.

VANDERGELDER:

I know I've been a fool about Mrs. Molloy, and that other woman. But, Dolly, forgive me and marry me.

He goes on his knees.

MRS. LEVI:

Horace, I don't dare. No. I don't dare.

VANDERGELDER:

What do you mean?

MRS. LEVI:

You know as well as I do that you're the first citizen of Yonkers. Naturally, you'd expect your wife to keep open house, to have scores of friends in and out all the time. Any wife of yours should be used to that kind of thing.

VANDERGELDER:

After a brief struggle with himself.

Dolly, you can live any way you like.

MRS. LEVI:

Horace, you can't deny it, your wife would have to be a *somebody*. Answer me: am I a somebody?

VANDERGELDER:

You are . . . you are. Wonderful woman.

MRS. LEVI:

Oh, you're partial.

She crosses, giving a big wink at the audience, and sits on sofa right.

VANDERGELDER *follows her on his knees.*

Horace, it won't be enough for you to load your wife with money and jewels; to insist that she be a benefactress to half the town.

He rises and, still struggling with himself, coughs so as not to hear this.

No, she must be a somebody. Do you really think I have it in me to be a credit to you?

VANDERGELDER:

Dolly, everybody knows that you could do anything you wanted to do.

MRS. LEVI:

I'll try. With your help, I'll try—and by the way, I found your purse.

Holds it up.

VANDERGELDER:

Where did you—! Wonderful woman!

MRS. LEVI:

It just walked into my hand. I don't know how I do it. Sometimes I frighten myself. Horace, take it. Money walks out of my hands, too.

VANDERGELDER:

Keep it. Keep it.

MRS. LEVI:

Horace!

Half laughing, half weeping, and with an air of real affection for him.

I never thought . . . I'd ever . . . hear you say a thing like that!

BARNABY *dashes in from the kitchen in great excitement. He has discarded Minnie's clothes.*

BARNABY:

Oh! Excuse me. I didn't know anybody was here.

VANDERGELDER:

Bellowing.

Didn't know anybody was here. Idiot!

MRS. LEVI:

Putting her hand on Vandergelder's arm; amiably:

Come in, Barnaby. Come in.

VANDERGELDER *looks at her a minute; then says, imitating her tone:*

VANDERGELDER:

Come in, Barnaby. Come in.

BARNABY:

Cornelius is going to marry Mrs. Molloy!!

MRS. LEVI:

Isn't that fine! Horace!. . .

MRS. LEVI *rises, and indicates that he has an announcement to make.*

VANDERGELDER:

Barnaby, go in and tell the rest of them that Mrs. Levi has consented—

MRS. LEVI:

Finally consented!

VANDERGELDER:

Finally consented to become my wife.

BARNABY:

Holy cabooses.

Dashes back to the doorway.

Hey! Listen, everybody! Wolf-trap—I mean—Mr. Vandergelder is going to marry Mrs. Levi.

MISS VAN HUYSEN *enters followed by all the people in this act. She is now carrying the box of chocolates.*

MISS VAN H.:

Dolly, that's the best news I ever heard.

She addresses the audience.

There isn't any more coffee; there isn't any more gingerbread; but there are three couples in my house and they're all going to get married. And do you know, one of those Ermengardes wasn't a dear little girl at all—she was a boy! Well, that's what life is: disappointment, illusion.

MRS. LEVI:
To audience.

There isn't any more coffee; there isn't any more ginger-bread, and there isn't any more play—but there is one more thing we have to do. . . . Barnaby, come here.

She whispers to him, pointing to the audience. Then she says to the audience:

I think the youngest person here ought to tell us what the moral of the play is.

BARNABY *is reluctantly pushed forward to the footlights.*

BARNABY:
Oh, I think it's about . . . I think it's about adventure. The test of an adventure is that when you're in the middle of it, you say to yourself, "Oh, now I've got myself into an awful mess; I wish I were sitting quietly at home." And the sign that something's wrong with you is when you sit quietly at home wishing you were out having lots of adventure. So that now we all want to thank you for coming tonight, and we all hope that in your lives you have just the right amount of sitting quietly at home, and just the right amount of . . . adventure. Goodnight!

MISS VAN HUYSEN *has been giving chocolates to the company—she now pops one into* BARNABY'S *mouth.*

THE
CURTAIN
FALLS

Afterword

———∿∿∿———

As Thornton Wilder stated clearly in the text of his play, *The Matchmaker* is "based upon" Johann Nestroy's 1842 Viennese satire, *Einen Jux will er sich machen* (awkwardly translated as "He Wants to Have a Fling"). Nestroy, who is often referred to as the Austrian Shakespeare, was in turn inspired by the English one-act play *A Day Well Spent* by John Oxenford (1835). Drawing for inspiration on a far more familiar work for English readers, Wilder also spliced into the middle of Act I of *The Matchmaker* an adapted short scene from Act II, Scene V of Molière's *L'Avare* (*The Miser*). In the scene, Molière's Frosine, the marriage broker, tries to interest Harpagon in a young woman's housekeeping and culinary skills, while in *Matchmaker*, Dolly Levi tries to interest Horace Vandergelder in the similar talents of Ernestina Simple. Thanks to this homage—which Wilder often recounted with glee (describing it by its official name of *Contaminatio*)— the roots of *The Matchmaker* can be traced directly to the Roman dramatist Plautus (254–184 BCE) and the dramatist Terence, a Roman of North African descent (185–159 BCE), thus providing a textbook example of the creative process as Wilder expressed it in his well-known Preface to

Three Plays: "Literature has always more resembled a torch race than a furious dispute among heirs."[*]

Putting the play's dramatic roots aside, the Broadway production of *The Matchmaker* was a dream come true for Wilder. The play had a 486-performance Broadway run in 1955–1956, a Wilder Broadway record (150 more performances than *Our Town*'s 336), followed by a recording-breaking five-month national tour. All this was preceded by a highly successful eight-month engagement on London's West End and was succeeded in turn by three successful works based on *Matchmaker*. Its most famous offspring by far was the internationally acclaimed, smash musical *Hello, Dolly!* (1964), a work that Wilder had no direct role in creating other than giving David Merrick the rights to fashion a musical. *The Matchmaker* also spawned two films, a 1958 adaptation of the original play with Shirley Booth, Anthony Perkins, and Shirley MacLaine, and the movie version of *Hello, Dolly!* starring Barbra Streisand and Walter Matthau.

The Matchmaker was legally embargoed for years at a time to provide an open road for *Hello, Dolly!* on stage and screen. Since 1972, when the last legal shackle was removed, the play has been available for licensing in the United States and Canada without any holdbacks and has been continuously revived professionally and served as a staple of school and community theater. It has also been produced in some fourteen countries in more than eleven languages. That said, when compared to the enormously popular *Our Town* and *Hello, Dolly!*, *The Matchmaker* is frequently and erroneously referred to by critics as a "rarely produced" work—ironically

---

[*] Please visit www.thorntonwilder.com to review Wilder's Preface to *Three Plays*. In addition to the Preface, *Three Plays*, first published in 1957, contains Wilder's definitive versions of *Our Town*, *The Skin of Our Teeth*, and *The Matchmaker*.

in tandem with a remark about how *The Matchmaker* makes them want to break into song.

The road to *The Matchmaker's* success was long and rocky, reaching a nadir when its first version, a four-act farce titled *The Merchant of Yonkers,* proved a flop on Broadway in 1939, closing after only thirty-nine performances. Wilder's persistence in bringing it to successful fruition attests not only to its inherent strengths from inception, but from the depth of its roots.

The creative cauldron of influences in *The Matchmaker* extend from Wilder's childhood relationship with the theater, to his passion for Moliere, farce, and German language and drama, through to his creative partnerships with practitioners whose work he admired and respected. As Wilder noted in his Preface to *Three Plays,* the foundations of this hydra-headed work were built during his boyhood encounters with the boisterous stock company productions he saw at the Ye Liberty Playhouse in Oakland, California. His youthful fascination with vaudeville and stage comedy led to his voracious reading of plays, his acting in Berkeley High School's annual vaudeville show, and his spending scores of hours in other theaters, including the University of California Berkeley's Greek Theatre near his home in the Berkeley Hills.

Early on in the course of his theatrical exploration, Moliere became one of Wilder's theatrical heroes. His technique is evident in Wilder's early three-minute plays (1915–1920) and in *Queens of France,* a one-act play published in 1931 that marked Wilder's arrival on the national scene as a serious dramatist. "*Queens of France* was written under *l'ombre de Molière*" Wilder wrote in 1930.

As a boy and young man, one of Wilder's great enthusiasms was collecting German theatrical data. This passion for German theater and knowledge of the German language precipitated his intimate acquaintance with the names and production histories of the leading German-speaking theaters, directors, and actors of the period. Among these names, Wilder likely encountered Viennese actor and playwright, Johann Nestroy (1801–1862) and the world-famous Austrian-born director and educator Max Reinhardt (1873–1943). These two figures would have a profound influence on the development of *The Matchmaker*. It is more than likely that young Wilder, who loved records and statistics, read the first influential study of Reinhardt published in this country in English, *The Theatre of Max Reinhardt* (1914), and came across a summary of Reinhardt's productions between 1903 and 1910 in the Appendix. There, on page 319, he would have discovered the name of the Nestroy play Reinhardt had mounted in 1904 at the Neues Theatre in Berlin: *Einen Jux will er sich machen*. Nestroy's satires were indelibly associated with Vienna's stage productions and argot but his work was still all but unknown in the United States in the 1930s.

Wilder sought Reinhardt out for the first time as early as 1923, at a theater in Philadelphia, and noted the meeting in a letter home with prophetic understatement. "A most valuable connection when I get back to playwriting," he wrote, in reference not only to the encounter but also to his first and deepest love, which he had put aside during this period to write fiction. Fittingly, his 1935 novel *Heaven's My Destination* demonstrated his interest in farce in prose terms. As he wrote in April 1934 to that novel's distinguished German translator, Herbert E. Herlitschka (one of Nestroy's fellow Austrians): "[Ferdinand] Raimund and Nestroy have become my great enthusiasm during the last two years and I should like to think that my book (though so far short

of those in literary merit) should nevertheless breathe that
loving saturation in the detailed atmosphere of a district
that is one of the great qualities of *Einen Jux will er sich
machen....*"

At last, Wilder was ready to attempt the play for which
he had been preparing for years. He began writing his
full-length farce in the summer of 1935. As he wrote to
his friend, the actress Ruth Gordon, in April 1936: "I've
been reading all the great 'formal' comedies in every language: Molière and Goldoni, and Lessing—just to make
sure that I've expunged every lurking vestige of what Sam
Behrman and George S. Kaufman think comedy is." The
play-in-progress was *The Merchant of Yonkers*, a farce appro-
priately listed in Wilder's records of this period as "Merchant
of Yonkers (Nestroy-Molière)." And from the beginning,
it is clear that he wanted Reinhardt to direct it. The dream
was hardly far-fetched; in the fall of 1934, the two men had
had long talks in Chicago (probably while Reinhardt was
directing *Midsummer Night's Dream*), at the end of which,
as Wilder informed his family, "with one hand on my shoulder [he] asked me to write a play for him. That was all; but I
walked on air."

At least one-half of *Merchant* was written in the same
period and in the same places as *Our Town* (the MacDowell
Colony in New Hampshire, ships at sea, and hotel rooms on
both sides of the Atlantic, to start a long list) and Wilder sent
Reinhardt, now a political refugee living in Los Angeles, the
first two acts shortly after *Our Town* opened on Broadway
on February 4, 1938. By early March, Wilder had fled to a
rented apartment in Tucson, Arizona to complete the work.
Here, by telegram, he learned the wonderful news that Reinhardt was "entzückt" (charmed) by what he had read. In
addition to Wilder's love affair with farce and Reinhardt's

interest in the play, the playwright now had another driving reason to complete *Merchant*. He had been surprised that *Our Town* left audiences feeling so sad, or, as he put it in a letter from Tucson to his friend and confidante Lady Sibyl Colefax in London, that *Our Town* "raises a devastating pessimism, a repudiation of the state of being alive." More than ever Wilder wanted to show how the stage could also be employed to make audiences laugh. Still, though *The Merchant of Yonkers* was a farce, Wilder wrote Colefax that he was also weaving into it "trenchant sparks of social comment," his polite way of describing the play's treatment of the effects of wealth on individual behavior and on society.

The importance of the "trenchant" theme in a work that celebrates such sacred ingredients of farce on the stage as disguises, mixed identities, hiding and leaping out of hidden places, and, of course, love, cannot be exaggerated. He wrote to Ruth Gordon (June 21, 1938) about Reinhardt's reception of his serious message with these words:

> In some trembling I read him the (new) monologue that Mrs. Levi has in Act IV and asked him whether it was not too earnest for the play. When I was finished he looked at his wife [actress Helene Thimig] and said in German: You see, he is a poet and turned to me and said: No, I have always said that in a comedy—and near the end—there should always be one moment of complete seriousness and by that the audience can see that also comedy parts are not just pastime.

By mid-July the acting drafts for Act III and IV had been typed and names of actors began to be tossed around for a play Reinhardt hoped to mount in Los Angeles, among them Mickey Rooney as Barnaby and Charles Boyer as Cornelius.

But nothing about theater is predictable. Because of a change in Reinhardt's schedule, theatrical producer Herman Shumlin arranged with The Theatre Guild for *Merchant* to be born the traditional way, in the East—an out-of-town tryout followed by a Broadway opening. After a short and frantic rehearsal period, a strategy not recommended for a theatrical form with as many tricky moving parts as farce, *The Merchant of Yonkers* opened in Boston in December. It was an omen for the disaster that lay ahead that the three top choices for the key role of Dolly—Dame Edith Evans, Ina Claire (a frequent in Behrman's plays), and even Wilder's friend and confidante Ruth Gordon—turned down the part. The producers were forced to settle on Jane Cowl (1883–1950), a headliner, but an actress whom they had initially passed over. Wilder's view of her before she was picked was that she "affected 'great lady' dignity unsuitable to us."

The Merchant of Yonkers premiered at Boston's Colonial Theatre on December 12, 1938. It faced a critical establishment walking on eggshells from having embarrassed itself by negatively misjudging and almost derailing *Our Town* on its path to Broadway less than a year earlier. While scribes found plenty to criticize, especially the play's pace (too slow), its length (too long), and the fact that many a line still had to be learned, they were determined to find the glass at least half full. The *Boston Globe* reported it "hilariously successful in places," and the *Christian Science Monitor* saw "an imaginative warmth that is rare in the theater."

Any hope that Wilder would have a third Broadway hit in two years (his adaptation of *A Doll's House* in 1937 and *Our Town* being the other two) died the morning after *Mer-*

chant opened on December 28 at Broadway's Guild Theatre. Some New York reviews were kind, but the burden of opinion spelled debacle. John Anderson wrote brutally in the *New York Journal-American*: "When a farce isn't funny, there is nothing to be done." Other reactions around town were that the play was "dull," "overly arch and tedious," "drugged boredom," possessed "little dexterity or finesse," and proved a "depressing spectacle." Jane Cowl was either panned for her performance or pitied for being associated with such a play. In addition to damning the production, several critics questioned the viability of the entire enterprise: "What in the name of God made a writer as exalted as Thornton Wilder think that it was important for him to wrench himself into the past to the extent of reviving a farce from the Vienna of 1842," wrote the unhappy Robert Benchley in *The New Yorker*.

Was *Merchant* fatally flawed? Wilder's close friend, the feisty critic and radio commentator Alexander Woollcott, to whom Wilder had dedicated *Our Town*, was confident the play was sound. He laid its failure at Reinhardt's door, accusing him of wrecking it with "heavy-handed" directing and poor casting. (Rumor has it that he came close to physically assaulting Reinhardt over the offense.) Even before it closed on Broadway Woollcott predicted to Wilder that the play would be successfully revived in a few years "in the American idiom." Students of Wilder and the play have echoed Woollcott's view ever since. Donald Haberman in his valuable work *The Plays of Thornton Wilder: A Critical Study* stated it this way:

> Reinhardt was expert at directing Nestroy's kind of play for German audiences, but he seemed to

understand neither Wilder's play nor the American crowd. His reputation depended on his creating style through elaborate stage effects and slow pace. . . . Wilder's play is not a period piece. To emphasize its time and place through visual effects is to destroy its immediacy, which is established in part by the delib- erate removal of all marks of any particular culture.

Wilder never shared this view completely. He believed that events of the time—the Depression and war jitters— rather than the production alone, played a significant role in the play's failure, and when the script was published in April 1939, he did not hesitate to dedicate it to Reinhardt with "deep admiration and indebtedness." Wilder's view was not a product of reflection after the carnage; the second day into the play's doomed run, he wrote his attorney: "It's all been worth it. The things that I've learned about playwriting; the association with Reinhardt; the gradual improvement of the text of this play which in its revival (1948) will be a nifty." And five years later, in September 1943, from his post with Air Force Intelligence in North Africa, the now Major Thornton Wilder wrote his sister regarding the ongo- ing interest in his farce: "I wish I were there to cut the play, and rebuild portions of it. Reviewing it in my memory. And started re-admiring Reinhardt so that I almost *signed up with him again.*"

Wilder, in fact, had to wait only a few months after *Mer- chant* closed on Broadway for a reassuring omen of what lay ahead: the play was published in April 1939 and soon after, schools, colleges, and community groups began per- forming it around the country. This pattern of "constant demand" (a phrase in Wilder's business correspondence), augmented by serious feelers for translation and film rights to the play even before the end of World War II, made it clear to Wilder's managers that the question of a revival was never whether, but when. Wilder's prediction of *Merchant*'s return to Broadway was off by seven years; in 1955, indeed, a very "nifty" revival did occur.

Ruth Gordon (1896–1986), whom Wilder deeply admired as an actress and adored as a human being, was responsible for the rebirth of *The Merchant of Yonkers* as *The Matchmaker*. With the determination of a "resolute lioness," as Wilder put it in his journal, Gordon began agitating for the project in early 1951 supported by her husband, playwright Garson Kanin and director Tyrone Guthrie. Wilder had originally written the part of Dolly Levi with Gordon in mind for the role, but she had turned it down, apparently not wishing to be directed by Reinhardt. Gordon's postwar plans for the play were canny: revive the work in London's West End, far from Broadway and any lingering memories of the earlier, ill-fated production. In addition, Gordon was well known on the London stage dating back to her 1936 triumph with Michael Redgrave in the Old Vic production of *The Country Wife*. (Gordon, who played Mrs. Pinchwife, was the first American actress to perform in that sacred space.) Gordon's wish was a happy command for Wilder. To clear the way for the new production, anticipated as early as the fall of 1952, he had his agents withdraw, until further notice, all new performance rights for the bubbling *Merchant* as of February 22, 1952. By May of that year, Tyrone Guthrie, who directed Gordon in *The Country Wife*, had signed on with enormous enthusiasm as its director. Inevitable delays occurred but by the fall of 1953, Ruth Gordon's faith in *Merchant* was rewarded by the decision of the Edinburgh

Festival (in its sixth year) to host the premiere in the summer of 1954, and of London's esteemed Tennent Productions, Ltd. to back it. Wilder's farce sailed into 1954 on a
sea of high and happy hopes. By January 1954, *The Merchant of Yonkers* also had a new name. At first a change was
thought unnecessary but it appears that the issue was forced
by lingering poor reviews from a 1952 North End London
production that had just escaped the play's embargo. In addition, Wilder was making a number of changes in the script.
On November 28, 1953, he wrote from Key West, Florida,
to Gordon and Kanin:

> Dear Sweetnesses:
> For a Title: How about
> THE MATCHMAKER. There's a title role for
> Ruthie. And a great help in Act II where the audi-
> ence will see more clearly why she's telling lies for
> and about Cornelius.
> If you don't like that, how about: THE GREEN
> SHOOTS or JOIN HANDS. Oh, dear—I want one
> that expresses the 'spring' out of bondage. The right
> to enjoyment. Isn't title-hunting tormenting?

Readers will recognize that the playwright's second and
third title choices spring directly from his statement in the
Preface to *Three Plays* that the play is about "the aspirations
of the young (and not only of the young) for a fuller, freer
participation in life."

It would be a mistake to say that the relaunching of
Merchant / Matchmaker was a cakewalk. Frayed nerves, tan-
trums, long nights devoted to rewriting and pruning and
cutting, and the fear of impending disaster are all part of

the play's story in Scotland and England. But Ruth Gordon and Tyrone Guthrie's instincts proved correct. The play Wilder called an "ugly duckling" opened on August 16, 1954, in the Theatre Royal in Newcastle-upon-Tyne for a six-performance "provincial city" tryout before its official debut at the Edinburgh Festival—and came away a swan. "It is a long time since there was a first night in Newcastle which pleased its audience to such a degree," wrote a reviewer. The show, even in this large theater, was a sellout by the third performance.

The Matchmaker did encounter a few harsh notices, typically from lordly big-city critics not fond of farce, and a few admonitions about tempo, timing, length, or the performance of a given actor. But starting in Newcastle, and going on to sixteen performances in Edinburgh, then to another ten weeks that fall in several additional provincial cities—even a dash to participate in another festival in Berlin—the production achieved success on an ever-larger and more glorious canvas. A sampling of praise gives the picture: the play was called "glittering" and "glowing," "frisky" and "sparkling," "like planting a telephone pole, and seeing it burst into leaves and chestnut candles." The London opening on November 4, 1954, at the Theatre Royal Haymarket—"charming," "delicious and elegant," "abounding high spirits"—was all but an anticlimax for this now field-tested, finely tuned farce. And give or take the few requisite moments of fear, panic, and temper, the story repeated itself later in the United States where, after two more fine-tunings in Philadelphia and Boston (now coproduced by David Merrick and The Theatre Guild), *The Matchmaker* commenced its "nifty" Broadway revival and run on December 5, 1955, with most of its original cast. Wilder was in Rome but the telegram he received the next morning from his dramatic agent, Harold

Freedman, left no doubt about what had occurred at the Royale Theater on Forty-Fifth Street:

AUDIENCE RECEPTION WONDERFUL [stop] NOTICES WONDERFUL [stop] LINE AT BOX OFFICE BEST HAROLD

Putting aside all questions of casting and rehearsal time, *The Matchmaker* was simply a different experience from *The Merchant of Yonkers*. The legendary stage publicist Richard Maney, who had handled the 1938 production, put the issue this way in 1957: "As played by Cowl and directed by Reinhardt, *The Merchant of Yonkers* was a roguish lark. Guthrie and Miss Gordon reduced it to bawdy slapstick." "Reduced" has negative connotations but what is clear is that slapstick "played" in 1954. *New York Times* critic Brooks Atkinson, a Wilder champion, felt compelled to write in 1938 about the play's "heavy feet." From London sixteen years later, he wrote enthusiastically about an event that "is broad and funny and seems a good deal more modern in spirit than machine-made goods like 'Anniversary Waltz' and 'The Tender Trap.'" Later, in New York, he would write admiringly of the play's "loud, vulgar, slapdash and uproarious" character. Did critics compare *Matchmaker* to *Merchant? Theatre Annual* phrased it this way: "[*The Matchmaker*] now careened where it once clattered and where it once sputtered, here exploded sky high."

What are the differences between *Merchant* and *Matchmaker?* In production, they came down largely to directorial interpretation. Guthrie's *Matchmaker* was resplendent with colorful and playful costumes and scenery. Reinhardt's *Merchant* had featured purples and period-piece furnishings. Guthrie's vision of the play and Gordon's interpretation of

Dolly Levi stood in sharp contrast to Reinhardt's more classical vision of how to mount farce and Jane Cowl's "great lady" performance. "This malevolent pixie," wrote the redoubtable Kenneth Tynan of Ruth Gordon's performance at the time of the London opening, "flies at the part like a bat out of hell"—and he and audiences loved her for it.

What of the two scripts? In letters written to his dramatic agent and attorney in July 1954 from rehearsals in London, Wilder described *The Matchmaker* as "extensively rewritten." But only three months later he saw it differently. On October 7, 1954, with the play approaching its London opening, he wrote his agent, "The wastepaper baskets of Europe are full of my rewriting." To clarify:

> Now here's the point of this letter—in all this rewriting what has happened is that the text has got back closer and closer to THE MERCHANT OF YONKERS. And that's natural: what I wrote in Arizona in 1938 was written when I had nothing else on my mind except THE MERCHANT. Now we change and change and finally it becomes clear that the original form was best. So when it's finally published or released . . . it will be evident to all that THE MATCHMAKER is merely a cut, trimmed, original, touched up YONKERS.

Wilder's view of the few differences between the two plays notwithstanding, the changes in *The Matchmaker* were significant enough to merit a new copyright. The two works were produced sixteen years apart with a depression and a war falling in between, so it is no surprise that we encounter different Americas and Americans in *Merchant* and *Match-*

maker. Two examples illustrate significant differences in language, tone, and staging. The first comes from Dolly Levi's soliloquy in Act IV. The Great Depression still had the country by the throat in 1938, with a host of schemes for collective political solutions in the wings. In what is all but a classroom lecture, Dolly addresses the audience in Act IV of *Merchant*:

> And the first sign that a person's refused the human race is that he makes plans to improve and restrict the human race according to patterns of his own.
> It looks like love of the human race, but believe me, it's the refusal of the human race—those blue-print worlds where everyone is supposed to be happy, and no one's allowed to be free.

In *The Matchmaker* of 1954, Dolly warns of the dangers of too much (or too little) money. But gone is the lecture. Instead, her speech is all but an aria of a lonely person ("a perfectly good oak leaf—but without color and without life") eager to rejoin the human race. And the comment about money—arguably the play's most famous line—now appears as: "Money, I've always felt, money—pardon my expression—is like manure; it's not worth a thing unless it's spread about encouraging young things to grow."

The second example is in the play's final words. Underscoring the principal theme of the play: aspirations of human beings for a "fuller, freer participation in life," Wilder concludes *The Matchmaker* by having Mrs. Levi ask Barnaby, the youngest member in the cast, for his opinion about the "moral of the play." In an increasingly enthusiastic eleven-line send-off commencing, "Oh, I think it's about . . . I think it's about adventure," Barnaby delivers the goods in the form of a personal testimony.

In sharp contrast, *The Merchant* concludes with a classic farce finale: the cast dances to a happy tune. The stage direction reads: *"The company has joined hands in a semi-circle and is singing 'Old Father Hudson,' as the curtain falls."*

The music for "Old Father Hudson" was composed for the show by the known team of Jack Green and Rowland V. Haas with lyrics contributed by none other than Thornton Wilder. This long lost piece of Wilder's artistic record follows:

> Some like a mountain side and some like the shore,
> Some like their deserts and keep asking for more;
> Give me a river, and a hill and a sky;
> I'll take the Hudson; there I'll live til I die.
> Call in the fiddlers three and put wood on blaze,
> Snow's on the Catskills and now short are the days;
> Out on the river there is ice on the shore,
> All merry Dutchmen start to stamp on the floor.
> [REFRAIN]
> OLD FATHER HUDSON, roll your waves to ocean!
> OLD FATHER HUDSON, roll your waves along!
> OLD FATHER HUDSON, roll your waves to ocean!
> OLD FATHER HUDSON, roll your waves along!
> All merry Dutchmen, living by your waters,
> All merry Dutchmen dance and sing this song.
> OLD FATHER HUDSON, from Troy to Staten Island,
> OLD FATHER HUDSON, roll your waves along!

What were Wilder's own views of the Guthrie-Gordon revival? He was glad and he was grateful. But the revised play was a learning experience for him, too. As rehearsals began in London, Wilder was temporarily thrown by watching his "happy little farce" subjected to a madcap interpretation. Shortly before the Newcastle opening, his sister wrote of his "agonizing experience" watching Guthrie "overdoing the play & losing it under a circus—the scenery & costumes belong in some other play. Miss G[ordon] is dashing around & screaming & waving her arms to suit herself." By the London opening, Wilder realized that Gordon's performance was "glorious" and, as he told his publisher, "made it an entirely new play." He also believed that the times favored the play. The postwar world was still at sixes and sevens but people were willing to laugh. "The earthquakes of Society have so altered the character of our time," Wilder thinks [as quoted in a wire story filed from Edinburgh after the opening] "that today comedy is the only means the theatre has to transmit a serious message." But it was a mark of Wilder's loyalty to the play's origins that he "again dedicated" it "to Max Reinhardt with deep admiration and indebtedness."

"If farce is a trivial untruth about life, our betters must be reprehended," Thornton Wilder wrote a Wellesley College theater company producing *Merchant* after World War II. Wilder remained proud to the end of his life for having contributed to an ancient and honorable theatrical tradition devoted to laughter. For this reason, no review of *Merchant/ Matchmaker* could have pleased him more than Walter Kerr's in the *New York Herald Tribune* the morning after its second coming on Broadway:

> Though he has nominally based his spectacular spree on a particular German comedy by Johann Nestroy,

184 ～ Afterword

he has actually been busy taking a veritable inventory
of the comic spirit, itemizing all the dives into cupboards, all the absurd uprushings of love, and even
all the picture-postcard settings that have ever done
duty in the cause of merriment.

TAPPAN WILDER
Sausalito, CA

Acknowledgments

———

NOTE ON SOURCES

The back matter for this volume is constructed in large part from Thornton Wilder's words in published material not easy to come by. Unless otherwise identified, all unpublished material and many of the news clips are from holdings in the Wilder Family Archives in the Yale Collection of American Literature in the Beinecke Rare Book and Manuscript Library at Yale (YCAL), or records held by the Wilder family. Wilder's legal and dramatic agency files have been especially useful sources for telling the story. When deemed appropriate, minor corrections of spelling, punctuation, and format have been made silently. Wilder's correspondence with Lady Sybil Colefax is held in Special Collections, The Fales Library & Special Collections at New York University, and his letters to Ruth Gordon by the Garson Kanin Estate.

PUBLICATIONS

The Reinhardt citation is from Huntly Carter's *The Theatre of Max Reinhardt* (New York: Mitchell Kennerley, 1914). Donald Haberman's quote is taken from *The Plays of Thornton Wilder: A Critical Study* (Middletown, Connecticut: Wesleyan University Press, 1967), 23; Richard Maney's from *Fanfare: The Confessions of a Press Agent* (New York: Harper & Row 1957), 329; and the quoted lines from *The Merchant of Yonkers* (New York: Harper & Brothers), 173, 180. Wilder's lyrics appeared in "Old Father Hudson" published by W. A. Quincke & Co., Hollywood, CA, 1939.

An earlier version of this Afterword appeared in the 2006 Harper-Collins edition of *Three Plays*. Since that time, two foundational works for understanding Thornton Wilder's life and art have been published by HarperCollins: Robin G. Wilder and Jackson R. Bryer edited *The Selected*

Letters of Thornton Wilder (2008) and Penelope Niven's definitive Wilder biography, *Thornton Wilder: A Life* (2012). Readers interested in learning more about Wilder are invited to consult these two important texts. We also invite readers to visit www.thorntonwilder.com for extensive materials including theater programs, photos, Wilder's 1938 essay, "Noting the Nature of Farce," his preface to *Three Plays*, and his Foreword to *Johann Nestroy: Three Comedies*, translated by Max Knight and Joseph Fabry (New York, Frederick Ungar Publishing Co., 1967). *The Beaux' Stratagem*, referenced in Ken Ludwig's Introduction, is published by Samuel French (2007), and *The Bride of Torozko* has not yet been published.

ACKNOWLEDGMENTS

I extend special thanks to Barbara Hogenson, Rosey Strub, and Jim Knable for their invaluable support in preparing this version of *The Matchmaker* Afterword. Sofia Groopman, the book's editor at HarperCollins, also deserves a special bow. Plaudits aside, I take full responsibility for errors and welcome corrections and comments.

Since 2003, ten notable novelists and playwrights have contributed Introductions to the HarperCollins editions of Thornton Wilder's novels and plays. The Wilder family is honored that Ken Ludwig accepted the invitation to join this group. To Ken goes a very deep bow.

TAPPAN WILDER

About the Author

In his quiet way, Thornton Niven Wilder was a revolutionary writer who experimented boldly with literary forms and themes, from the beginning to the end of his long career. "Every novel is different from the others," he wrote when he was seventy-five. "The theater (ditto). . . . The thing I'm writing now is again totally unlike anything that preceded it." Wilder's richly diverse settings, characters, and themes are at once specific and global. Deeply immersed in classical as well as contemporary literature, he often fused the traditional and the modern in his novels and plays, all the while exploring the cosmic in the commonplace. In a January 12, 1953, cover story, *Time* took note of Wilder's unique "interplanetary mind"—his ability to write from a vision that was at once American and universal.

A pivotal figure in the history of twentieth-century letters, Wilder was a novelist and playwright whose works continue to be widely read and produced in this new century. He is the only writer to have won the Pulitzer Prize for both Fiction and Drama. His second novel, *The Bridge of San Luis Rey,* received the Fiction award in 1928, and he won the prize twice in Drama, for *Our Town* in 1938 and *The Skin of Our Teeth* in 1943. His other novels are *The Cabala, The Woman of Andros, Heaven's My Destination, The Ides of March, The Eighth Day,* and *Theophilus North.* His other major dramas include *The Matchmaker,* which was adapted as the internationally acclaimed musical comedy *Hello, Dolly!,* and *The Alcestiad.* Among his innovative shorter plays are *The Happy*

Journey to Trenton and Camden and *The Long Christmas Dinner,* and two uniquely conceived series, *The Seven Ages of Man* and *The Seven Deadly Sins,* frequently performed by amateurs.

Wilder and his work received many honors, highlighted by the three Pulitzer Prizes, the Gold Medal for Fiction from the American Academy of Arts and Letters, the Order of Merit (Peru), the Goethe-Plakette der Stadt (Germany, 1959), the Presidential Medal of Freedom (1963), the National Book Committee's first National Medal for Literature (1965), and the National Book Award for Fiction (1968).

He was born in Madison, Wisconsin, on April 17, 1897, to Amos Parker Wilder and Isabella Niven Wilder. The family later lived in China and in California, where Wilder graduated from Berkeley High School. After two years at Oberlin College, he went on to Yale, where he received his undergraduate degree in 1920. A valuable part of his education took place during summers spent working hard on farms in California, Kentucky, Vermont, Connecticut, and Massachusetts. His father arranged these rigorous "shirtsleeve" jobs for Wilder and his older brother, Amos, as part of their initiation into the American experience.

Thornton Wilder studied archaeology and Italian as a special student at the American Academy in Rome (1920–1921), and earned a master of arts degree in French literature at Princeton in 1926.

In addition to his talents as playwright and novelist, Wilder was an accomplished teacher, essayist, translator, scholar, lecturer, librettist, and screenwriter. In 1942, he teamed with Alfred Hitchcock to write the first draft of the screenplay for the classic thriller *Shadow of a Doubt,* receiving credit as principal writer and a special screen credit for his "contribution to the preparation" of the production. All but fluent in four languages, Wilder translated and adapted plays by such varied authors as Henrik Ibsen, Jean-Paul Sartre, and André Obey. As a scholar, he conducted significant research on James Joyce's *Finnegans Wake* and the plays of Spanish dramatist Lope de Vega.

Wilder's friends included a broad spectrum of figures on both sides of the Atlantic—Hemingway, Fitzgerald, Alexander Woollcott, Gene Tunney, Sigmund Freud, producer Max Reinhardt, Katharine Cornell, Ruth Gordon, and Garson Kanin. Beginning in the mid-1930s, Wilder was especially close to Gertrude Stein and became one of her most effective interpreters and champions. Many of Wilder's friendships are documented in his prolific correspondence. Wilder believed that great letters constitute a "great branch of literature." In a lecture titled "On Reading the Great Letter Writers," he wrote that a letter can function as a "literary exercise," the "profile of a personality," and "news of the soul," apt descriptions of thousands of letters he wrote to his own friends and family.

Wilder enjoyed acting and played major roles in several of his own plays in summer theater productions. He also possessed a lifelong love of music; reading musical scores was a hobby, and he wrote the librettos for two operas based on his work: *The Long Christmas Dinner,* with composer Paul Hindemith, and *The Alcestiad,* with composer Louise Talma. Both works premiered in Germany.

Teaching was one of Wilder's deepest passions. He began his teaching career in 1921 as an instructor in French at Lawrenceville, a private secondary school in New Jersey. Financial independence after the publication of *The Bridge of San Luis Rey* permitted him to leave the classroom in 1928, but he returned to teaching in the 1930s at the University of Chicago. For six years, on a part-time basis, he taught courses there in classics in translation, comparative literature, and composition. In 1950–1951, he served as the Charles Eliot Norton Professor of Poetry at Harvard. Wilder's gifts for scholarship and teaching (he treated the classroom as all but a theater) made him a consummate, much-sought-after lecturer in his own country and abroad. After World War II, he held special standing, especially in Germany, as an interpreter of his own country's intellectual traditions and their influence on cultural expression.

During World War I, Wilder had served a three-month stint as an enlisted man in the Coast Artillery section of the army, stationed at Fort Adams, Rhode Island. He volunteered for service in World War II, advancing to the rank of lieutenant colonel in Army Air Force Intelligence. For his service in North Africa and Italy, he was awarded the Legion of Merit, the Bronze Star, the Chevalier Légion d'Honneur, and honorary officership in the Military Order of the British Empire (M.B.E.).

From royalties received from *The Bridge of San Luis Rey,* Wilder built a house for his family in 1930 in Hamden, Connecticut, just outside New Haven. But he typically spent as many as two hundred days a year away from Hamden, traveling to and settling in a variety of places that provided the stimulation and solitude he needed for his work. Sometimes his destination was the Arizona desert, the MacDowell Colony in New Hampshire, or Martha's Vineyard, Newport, Saratoga Springs, Vienna, or Baden-Baden. He wrote aboard ships, and often chose to stay in "spas in off-season." He needed a certain refuge when he was deeply immersed in writing a novel or play. Wilder explained his habit to a *New Yorker* journalist in 1959: "The walks, the quiet—all the elegance is present, everything is there but the people. That's it! A spa in off-season! I make a practice of it."

But Wilder always returned to "the house *The Bridge* built," as it is still known to this day. He died there of a heart attack on December 7, 1975.